"It's Dub Dugan!" a female voice called out, and Hart turned to see a woman and a small girl hurrying toward them across the parking lot.

"Where's your hat?" the girl asked.

Hart felt himself break out into a sweat. Dub had promised not to wear the hat.

"My hat?" Dub boomed. "You want to see my hat?" He began to pretend to look for the hat. "Is it under here?" He bent to look under the car.

"No!" the girl squealed.

"Is it here?" He looked behind the girl's ear. She squealed again.

Hart froze. He knew what was coming now. He shrank back against the station wagon.

"Well . . . maybe . . ." Dub said, his hand on the door handle, "it's in here!" The rear door flew open. Out came the hat. Before Hart could catch his breath it was on Dub's head.

Ta ta ta ta ta TA.

Dub danced in the parking lot. His arms rolled in one direction. His hip threw out in the other direction. The fruit bobbed. The ribbons flew. The girl squealed with delight. Hart's mouth dropped open at the horror of it.

His worst nightmare had come true.

OTHER PUFFIN BOOKS YOU MAY ENJOY

COASTER

by Betsy Duffey

PUFFIN BOOKS

PUFFIN BOOKS
Published by the Penguin Group
Penguin Books USA Inc., 375 Hudson Street, New York, New York 10014, U.S.A.
Penguin Books Ltd, 27 Wrights Lane, London W8 5TZ, England
Penguin Books Australia Ltd, Ringwood, Victoria, Australia
Penguin Books Canada Ltd, 10 Alcorn Avenue, Toronto, Ontario, Canada M4V 3B2
Penguin Books (N.Z.) Ltd, 182-190 Wairau Road, Auckland 10, New Zealand
Penguin Books Ltd, Registered Offices: Harmondsworth, Middlesex, England

First published in the United States of America by Viking, a division of
Penguin Books USA Inc., 1994
Published in Puffin Books, 1996

1 3 5 7 9 10 8 6 4 2

THE LIBRARY OF CONGRESS HAS CATALOGED THE VIKING EDITION AS FOLLOWS:
Duffey, Betsy.
Coaster/Betsy Duffey.
p. cm.
Summary: While secretly building a roller coaster in the woods, twelve-year-old
Hart tries to come to terms with his parents' divorce and his mother's
new relationship with a television weatherman.
ISBN 0-670-85480-8
[1. Divorce—Fiction. 2. Roller coasters—Fiction.] I. Title.
PZ7.D876Co 1994
[Fic]—dc20 94-6487
CIP AC

Puffin Books ISBN 0-14-036956-2
Printed in the United States of America

For my brave father, with love

Contents

Contents

COASTER

The Wild Side

"Dare you."

"What?" Hart looked at his father, then out the car window at the old roller coaster. He blinked.

"Dare you," his father said again, nodding toward the coaster.

Hart didn't unbuckle his seat belt. "I thought we were taking me to get my school clothes. Mom said . . ."

A train passed over the nearest hump of the coaster and they heard boards rattle and people scream.

"You listen to your mother too much," his father said. His eyes glittered with excitement. "School clothes can wait. Come on, Hart. Let's do it."

Hart's father jumped out of the old MG convertible without opening the door. He leaned back against the red hood and looked up at the old wooden coaster.

It was a classic woodie called the Wild Side—a coaster built of wooden beams supporting rickety metal tracks. The whitewashed beams stretched out for at least a quarter of a mile, rolling like waves along the boardwalk.

Everywhere it was metal, it was rusted. Everywhere it was painted, it was peeling.

"I haven't been on one of those since I was your age. My brother and I used to ride the Cyclone at Coney Island."

Hart could easily imagine his father on the coaster with Uncle Mark. They both loved thrills and danger, and the Wild Side looked dangerous. It was old, rickety, unsafe.

Hart unbuckled his seat belt and got out of the car. "School starts tomorrow," he called to his father's back. "I've got to have—"

Beams creaked. Wheels screeched on rusty metal tracks.

"Later," his father called over his shoulder. He was already halfway across the parking lot, striding with determination toward the park entrance.

Hart followed helplessly, thinking of his mother back at the house. It was the first time she had let him go with his father since the divorce. She would be disappointed if they came home without his new clothes.

He looked around nervously at the seedy gift shops and at the beer cans littering the ground. His mother had never allowed him to go to the boardwalk—too dangerous. He could almost hear her voice saying, *"Don't touch anything!"* She had saved an article from the newspaper when two students had been hurt Bungee jumping at the boardwalk, another when a man was robbed here at gunpoint.

Hart stepped up to the ticket booth. His father was already buying the tickets. "Unlimited rides," his father read from the back of the tickets.

"One will be plenty," said Hart. He had never been on a coaster before. The rumbling was louder now.

"One," said his father, "is never enough."

They moved toward the line, his father leading the way. The coaster grew before their eyes as they walked closer and closer to the loading station.

"You afraid?" his father asked.

"No," Hart answered. His voice cracked a little and gave him away. He wasn't good at lying.

His father's hand settled on Hart's thin shoulder as they hurried forward. "We die—we die together," he said.

Hart tried to laugh but it caught in his throat.

They walked up onto the ramp. The attendant opened a small gate and they got on the coaster side by side. The car was old and beat-up. It smelled of machine oil and hot metal and sweat. The padding on the sides of the car was cracked and slashed, patched with pieces of silver duct tape.

"Here goes nothing," said his father as the car eased out of the station. They rolled about twenty feet, then caught on the lift chain and jerked forward and upward.

His father squeezed the back of Hart's neck as they were pulled up the lift.

No turning back.

They pulled up twenty feet.

Thirty.

Forty.

The ticket booth and the parking lot were far below them. Hart looked out over the town. He could almost see the shopping center where they had been headed.

Fifty.

Sixty.

Seventy.

Hart looked down to see if he could spot the MG. His stomach lurched as he saw it. A toy car far below.

Then they dropped.

They plunged down the first hill out of control, screaming together. The cars jerked and bumped on the metal tracks, and they were thrown back and forth, beaten against the sides of the car. The metal restraining bar cut against their knees.

Going around a curve a hundred feet above the ground, Hart hit the wooden side once and felt it give a little. For a second he had an image of the side popping open and sending him flying out over the ocean like a watermelon seed squeezed between two fingers. He held tight to the bar and felt the reassuring bump of his father's shoulder against his.

He heard his father beside him shouting, "Woah! Woah!" and an occasional "Yeeow!"

Hart screamed with him.

Halfway through the ride, at the point where the cars dipped toward a tunnel, there was a cross beam just above the track.

Hart felt the dip and heard the swish of air as the cross beam passed over his head, and he squeezed his eyes shut. He did not want to see. He gripped the restraining bar with both fists, knuckles white. The screams echoed louder around him in the tunnel—his own scream the loudest in his ears.

They rolled into the station and got out of the car on wobbly legs. Hart's throat was tight from shouting.

He looked at his father, who was resting his hands on his knees trying to catch his breath. His father returned his look with a grin. Hart grinned back, and without a word they both began to run out the exit to the back of the line to ride the Wild Side again.

As they pulled up the lift hill for the second ride, his father poked Hart in the side with an elbow. "Open 'em!" he yelled.

Hart kept his eyes open. He saw his father grinning into the wind, his hair blowing straight back. He saw the first plunge. He saw the cross beam and the tunnel. His father held up his hands. Hart raised his too. Two skinny arms beside two strong ones.

After a few rides, Hart began to get the feel of the coaster. There was a skill to riding a coaster, like the skill of riding a horse. Once he relaxed, he learned to ride *with* the movement of the coaster instead of *against* it.

Yeeow!

They rode again and again, yelling together, until the sun dipped low in the sky and the string of Christmas-tree lights on the coaster began to twinkle. As they walked down the ramp after the final ride a flashbulb exploded in their faces.

"Five bucks," the man said as the photograph slid out of the camera. "For a memory." He smiled expectantly and held out the photo.

Hart's father dug into his pocket and produced a crumpled five-dollar bill. He gave it to the man and handed Hart the photo.

Before their eyes, it developed. First the coaster in the background. The web of whitewashed beams. Then the two of them in front, the color filling in, until they stared, complete, out of the photo.

His father was glowing. His square chin jutted forward framing a big grin. His black wavy hair was windblown from the coaster. His hand was on Hart's shoulder.

Hart beamed out. The same square jaw. The same grin. Bony arms and bony legs next to his father's strong ones.

Coaster partners.

As they hurried back to the car the sun was setting. The stores were all closed but now Hart didn't care.

"Hey, look," his father called out happily. "They put a bumper sticker on the car."

Hart hurried around to the back to read it.

"My motto!" his father said.

The bumper sticker seemed to sum up his father's attitude toward life in one sentence:

RIDE ON THE WILD SIDE!

The Backyard Coaster

Hart sat on his bed staring at the picture of the Wild Side. The color had faded slightly. Could it have been only two years ago? He saw himself at ten, his own wide-open grin, and wondered that he had ever looked so happy.

In the picture Hart's smile was like his father's; it *was* his father's. And the shape of his face—he traced it with his fingers—it was the shape of his father's face. They both had the same square chin and narrow nose. The black wavy hair was the same.

Only their eyes were different. His father's crystal-blue eyes seemed to burn with a fire behind them. His own were a deep brown like his mother's eyes but framed with wire-rimmed glasses.

His mother thought he was handsome. The girls in his class called him "Hart-throb," but he hated the way he looked.

The Wild Side still stood majestically in the background. But everything else had changed.

"Open up!"

Frankie Cambardella's round face peered into Hart's bedroom window. A circle of steam blew onto the glass from Frankie's breath. Hart dropped the picture onto his bed and hurried over to the window.

"Come on! Come on! It's freezing out here." Frankie rubbed his arms as Hart pulled up the window. Frankie threw one leg up, wedged his stomach over the sill, and flopped onto the floor like a beached whale. He sat up and stretched his T-shirt back into place and straightened his Phillies cap. Mrs. Cambardella always cut Frankie's hair herself and as far as Frankie was concerned the baseball cap was a necessity rather than a fashion statement.

"He here yet?" Frankie got to his feet, brushing off his faded jeans.

Hart shook his head. "Not yet."

Frankie picked up a newspaper clipping from the bed. The photo of a roller coaster seemed to jump from the page. It showed a single loop, the inverted train curled just at the peak of the arc. Riders with their hands up, their faces frozen in expressions somewhere between fear and bliss, were framed by the giant circle of steel.

"So, when do you leave?"

"Soon," Hart answered. "*Too* soon."

"Wow," Frankie said as he studied the picture on the newspaper clipping. "You sure he won't let you take a friend along?"

Hart shook his head. "We're supposed to 'get to know each other,' " he said.

"Why now? You've known him for almost three months."

"My mom thinks I don't like him. She thinks we need to spend more time together." Hart looked at the picture on the clipping. "In less than two hours I'll be there."

Frankie lifted his hands into the air, raised his feet, and opened his mouth to pantomime a scream like the people in the picture. "Hey," he said, "you should be happy your mom's dating a celebrity. At least you get to go to Wonderworld. Get him to buy you stuff. Mothers' boyfriends are great for that."

"I wouldn't call it dating," Hart said. "And I wouldn't call Dub Dugan a celebrity." It irritated him when people referred to Dub as a celebrity.

Once Hart had gone out to dinner with his mother and Dub, and everyone in the restaurant had recognized Dub. Dub spent the whole dinner waving to people and passing out WBST pencils. Frankie, whose goal in life was to be a professional wrestler, obviously did not appreciate the fact that some people did not like to be noticed.

"My friend going to Wonderworld with a famous person. It's too much." Frankie put his hand to his head as if to take it in.

"Lay off, Frankie, he's just a weatherman."

"*Just* a weatherman. Is the Mona Lisa *just* a painting? He's the *ultimate* weatherman. Did you see it last week when he wore the hat with the fruit on it?"

Hart nodded miserably. "He wears it whenever it's going to be sunny out. It's his 'tropical look.' Then he does a dance step."

"Oh yeah," Frankie said. "Like this."

Frankie rolled his hands around each other then lifted one into the air. As he lifted his hand he threw his hip out to the side. "*Ta ta ta ta ta TA!*"

Hart laughed. "I think it's more like this. *Ta ta ta ta ta TA!*" He rolled his hands around each other and when he lifted one hand he kicked to the back.

Frankie laughed too. "I wonder what he'll wear today," he said. "It *is* sunny out."

Hart stopped laughing.

"The hat with the fruit on it?" Frankie said.

"Surely he wouldn't," Hart said.

"Or the hula skirt? Hey, one time he wore a Shirley Temple wig," said Frankie.

"No!"

"I swear," said Frankie. "It was made out of corks from a wine festival."

Hart sat down. He was tired of talking about Dub.

"Do you want the good news now or later?" he asked Frankie to change the subject.

"What good news? Tell me. Tell me."

"The workmen building the McGinnitys' house are going to give us the leftover wood."

Frankie's face brightened. "You know what this means?" he said excitedly.

Hart nodded. "We can finish the Termite after I get back tonight." He gave a warning look toward the closed door.

"I'll take the plans," said Frankie. "You can meet me over there when you get home."

Hart gave the door another look, then pulled a worn-looking roll of paper out from under the bed. He carefully rolled it out onto the bed. It looked like a blueprint of a house but the design was more like some kind of mechanical snake. At the top were the words THE TERMITE—A BACKYARD COASTER.

"Hart," his mother called from the living room. "Dub just phoned. He's on his way over."

Hart quickly began to roll up the plan.

"He's on his way here!" Frankie said in an excited voice. "How long does it take him to get here?"

"Just a few minutes," said Hart. "He lives in one of those new apartments across the interstate."

"I've got to see what he's wearing."

"I'll tell you later," said Hart. He handed the plan to Frankie. "My mom will get mad if she knows you're here. You're a bad influence on me, you know."

Frankie grinned.

"Remember everything about the Jaguar," Frankie said. "And come over as soon as you get back." He put one leg over the windowsill and disappeared.

Hart picked up the collection of pictures and newspaper clippings and put them into a shoe box. He tucked the box under his bed and sat on the bed to wait for Dub, feeling like a prisoner waiting for his execution.

Finally a car door slammed outside.

"Hart*well!*" his mother called. Hart cringed. His mother only used his real name as a kind of warning. "Dub's here."

Slowly Hart left his room and headed down the hall.

"There you are!" Hart's mother said as he walked into the living room. She held a small shaggy poodle under each arm. Dub sat in an armchair looking at one of his mother's parenting magazines.

"You've got everything, Hart?" his mother asked.

"Yeah."

She followed him as he walked across the living room to the front door. "That jacket's warm enough?"

"Yes, Mom."

"Have you got enough money?"

"He won't need any money, Sandra," Dub said. "It's my treat."

Dub rose from the chair and came toward them. He

seemed to glide forward across the room like a parade float. The man had on a suit and *tie*. The tie was bright blue with clouds on it.

The hula skirt might have been better than this, Hart thought. Dub would be the only person in the history of Wonderworld to come wearing a suit and tie.

"I just wish I could go along," Hart's mother said wistfully.

"Well, come with us," said Dub.

She shook her head. The curly brown ponytail on top of her head bounced. Two silver earrings in the shape of tiny dog biscuits swung back and forth.

"You know I have these poodles to clip."

The two shaggy-looking dogs were panting with fear. One gave a whine.

"Next time," Dub said soothingly. He put his arm around her slender shoulders.

Hart had the terrible feeling that Dub was going to lean over the poodles and kiss his mother right there in front of him. He turned quickly, bumping Dub out of the way. As he turned, he caught sight of the mail truck out the window.

"Oh, there's the mail," he said, pleased with the timing. "I'm expecting a letter"—he paused for effect—"from my dad."

"Oh, Hartwell," his mother said in a disappointed way. Hart felt a glimmer of satisfaction. His mother did not like for him to talk about his dad in front of

Dub. If only the letter would come now. His mother and Dub seemed to forget that he even had a father at all.

"I'll be right back." He hurried outside down the steps and waved to the woman in the mail truck as he ran across the lawn. Hart took the letters and flipped quickly through the small pile of bills, magazines, and junk mail. He looked in vain for hotel stationery, his father's brisk handwriting—but nothing. Slowly he walked back up the path to the house.

"This is so nice of you, Dub," his mother was saying as they walked out onto the porch. "I know you don't care one thing about roller coasters."

"I never said that."

"But to drive two hours . . ."

Hart handed the mail to his mother. "The letter will probably come Monday. Every summer," he added to Dub, "my dad and I go coastering."

"That so?" said Dub.

"That's why I ran to get the mail. He writes to tell me where we're going. He—"

"Well," his mother interrupted, "you two better get going."

"Ready?" said Dub. He rubbed his hands together. "Let's get to that coaster. What do you call that thing? The Leopard?"

"The Jaguar." Hart moved toward Dub's station wagon, opened the door, and climbed inside. As he slid

into the seat he saw it. A large pile of straw and frui
and ribbons lay on the backseat—the hat.

Dub slipped behind the wheel. Hart's mother and the
poodles watched from the doorway as they backed ou
into the street. His mother made one of the poodle
wave. Dub chuckled. He honked the horn twice and
waved back. "Wonderworld or bust!" he called out the
window.

Hart closed his eyes and slumped lower into the
seat.

Hart's Worst Nightmare

"You're not very much like my dad," Hart said. He crossed his arms and tucked his hands into his armpits. Body language. He had learned that from one of his mother's parenting magazines. Crossed arms sent a negative message to the other person. It was the same as saying, "I don't like you," only without the words.

"Probably not." Dub came to a full stop at the corner and put on the blinker to turn.

"Like, my dad loves coasters. He really knows how to ride a coaster. You ever ridden a coaster?"

Dub shook his head. The car eased forward.

Without warning the vision of Dub on a coaster came into Hart's mind. He could imagine Dub in the hat, going over the first hill. He could see the ribbons trailing out behind Dub in the breeze and Dub's face frozen in a scream. No hair would be blowing in the wind. He tried to get a close look at Dub's hair. It was a mixture of gray and black, and there was a lot more of it around the sides than on the top.

His father, on the other hand, had plenty of hair. It was thick and wavy like Hart's. He ran his fingers through his own hair.

"Nope." Dub turned the car onto the ramp of the interstate highway. "I've never been on a coaster."

"Never?"

"I don't like to go fast. I don't like to go high. And I don't like to go upside down." He chuckled. "How do you ride a coaster, anyway?"

"Well," said Hart, "most people grab the bar."

"Sounds good to me," said Dub. "Grab it tight?"

"No, no," said Hart. "You shouldn't grab the bar at all, you should relax. You keep your arms free for lifting. Going down a hill at sixty miles per hour is just like flying!"

Dub let out a low whistle. "Okay. What else?"

"The only thing better than holding your arms up," Hart continued, "is lifting your feet up too." He looked over at Dub to see his reaction. Dub was nodding. His eyes, focused on the road ahead, crinkled in an amused grin.

"And of course, you never close your eyes."

"I'll try to keep that in mind," said Dub. "I'm pretty good at riding the merry-go-round. I always keep my eyes open!"

Cars zoomed past them. They crept along at just the

speed limit. Hart tried to imagine Dub on the Jaguar. Dub would be a white-knuckler for sure. That's what Hart's father called people who gripped the lap bar so tightly that their knuckles turned white. He remembered for a moment his own first ride on the Wild Side. He didn't like to admit, even to himself, that he had once been a white-knuckler. Now he was an expert rider.

Hart took a closer look at the hat on the backseat. It was straw with plastic pieces of fruit wired onto it. Apples, bananas, and bunches of grapes. He imagined Dub walking into the Wonderworld entrance in the hat, doing the dance step like Frankie had.

A conga line of dancing people would form behind Dub. *Ta ta ta ta ta TA!* It would be a nightmare. His worst nightmare. How could he tell Dub not to wear the hat? He had to say *something.*

"Also," Hart said, "some people don't know how to *dress* for coaster riding." He looked pointedly at Dub's suit and tie.

"Oh?" said Dub. "How do you dress for a coaster?"

"Glasses guard." Hart wiggled his. "Very important for loop-the-loops."

"I can imagine," said Dub.

"Jeans, comfortable shoes." He wiggled his feet. "And an *appropriate* shirt." He opened his jacket to show his T-shirt. It said RAISE YOUR HANDS IF YOU LOVE COASTERS!

"Nice," said Dub.

"And most important of all . . ." Hart paused. "No hats."

"Oh?" Dub's eyes crinkled again.

"Like, my dad wouldn't wear a hat to ride coasters."

"Oh?" Dub smiled.

"Like, a hat might blow off . . . or . . . it might get caught in the machinery . . . say . . . if it had ribbons on it."

Dub didn't answer. He obviously was not getting the message. The smile turned into a grin.

"My dad wouldn't wear a hat with fruit on it," Hart blurted out.

"Well," Dub replied, chuckling, "I don't plan to either."

"You don't?"

"Of course I don't. You don't think I want to embarrass you, do you?"

Hart gave a sigh of relief. "I didn't really think you would."

"Of course not. The hat's for later."

"Later?"

"I wear the hat at Scottish Rite, the children's hospital, as one of their hospital clowns. The hat looks pretty silly, but it serves a purpose."

"Like what?" Hart could not think of any purpose worth wearing a hat with fruit on it.

"Some of the kids feel so bad that they like to see a goofy-looking guy in a hat. It cheers them up."

Hart didn't reply. Instead he rested his head against the cool window and pretended to doze. Closed eyes were surely body language for *Leave me alone*.

He could be home right now working on the Termite with Frankie. Today they could have finished it.

He remembered the day that he found the coaster plans in a catalog called *Things You Never Knew You Needed*. The ad had been right between the ads for a *Star Trek: The Next Generation* uniform and a remote-control whoopie cushion.

The picture of the coaster in the ad had surprised him with its simplicity. A long track of boards, lined up end to end, stretched down a mountain, following the natural slope of the hill. A two-inch-wide board was nailed down the center of the track to hold the cart on the tracks. There was a boy riding on the coaster, smiling and waving.

The hill in the picture had looked a lot like the ravine back in the woods that were behind Frankie's house. It was the kind of thing his father would love. It was, in a word, perfect.

Hart's hand had been shaking with excitement as he filled out the order blank. He hurried to the post office the next day to get the money order with his allowance to send with the order. He waited weeks for the plans to come, worried that his mother would see the package in the mail before he could hide it.

She would not approve of his building a roller coaster. She had taken a class in Child Safety the year that he was born, and now he was the only twelve-year-old kid in town whose house still had safety locks on the cabinets.

She still worried that he would get suffocated by a plastic dry-cleaning bag or get food poisoning from mayonnaise. She would not even let him use a hammer unsupervised—much less build a roller coaster.

Before the divorce, her concern had been mostly for his father. "Where are you going?" she would say to Kip. "Why can't you stay at home with us?" Now that he was gone there was only Hart, and she focused her entire maternal concern on him.

Dub tapped a rhythm on the steering wheel as they drove toward Wonderworld. "Forty more miles," he said to Hart.

Hart didn't answer. He opened his eyes and stared out the window at the scenery, remembering the day his mother had met Dub. Hart had been helping his mother with the dogs that day. They had already washed and clipped three poodles, an Airedale, and a Lhasa apso when the doorbell rang. His mother groaned. "Not another one," she said. "Hart, if that's another dog . . ."

"I'll get it!" Hart hurried to the door, afraid that it might be the mailman with his coaster plans. It was not the mailman. It *was* another dog, and a man. A man in a starched white shirt. A man who looked familiar.

"Is this Sandra's Classic Clips?"

"Yes," said Hart, relieved.

"I know I don't have an appointment. But . . . my regular groomer closed and I wanted to do the weather with Doobie tonight." That's why the man looked familiar; Hart had seen him on the news. "I think it's going to rain cats and dogs tomorrow," he added with a wink. "So can you do one more dog?" He was holding a nervous-looking poodle under one arm.

Hart hesitated, and then his mother walked out into the living room. "I'm full up today," she began, but when she saw Dub, she broke off and smiled. "Well, there's always room for one more," she said. Hart's mouth dropped open in surprise as she took the poodle.

Later that night, dinner sat getting cold on the dining room table while they watched the weather report on TV.

"Let's eat, Mom."

"Just a minute. I want to see this." She had stared at

the TV, her eyes intense in the blue light, watching Dub talking in front of a large weather map.

When Doobie made his appearance on the screen in a tiny yellow raincoat, she began to laugh so hard that tears streamed down her face. Hart had not heard her *really* laugh since the divorce.

After the weather report, Hart went back to thinking about the coaster plans. He had not known at the time that his mother was making plans of her own. Plans with Dub.

"Here we are!" called Dub.

Hart blinked and looked out the window again, and then Dub was forgotten as he scanned the skyline for the Jaguar. A ripple of excitement ran through him. Where was it?

"There she blows!" said Dub.

They turned into the parking lot and there was the Jaguar in the distance. Hart followed it with his eyes as they drove in the line of cars to the first available parking spaces. They parked beside a pole with a blue hippo on it. "Remember Hippo," said Dub. He turned off the engine and, looking in the rearview mirror, straightened his tie.

Hart got out and stretched, never taking his eyes off the coaster. He was already imagining the view from the top of the lift hill.

"Ready?" asked Dub.

"Ready," answered Hart.

"It's Dub Dugan!" a female voice called out, and Hart turned to see a woman and a small girl hurrying toward them across the parking lot.

"Dub!" the little girl called. She ran with her arms extended. "Dub!"

Dub reached down and hugged the girl.

"She was in Scottish Rite," said the mother when she reached them. "She's never forgotten you, Mr. Dugan."

"Where's your hat?" the girl asked.

Hart could see the hat lying on the backseat of the car and he felt himself break out into a sweat. Dub had promised not to wear the hat.

"My hat?" Dub boomed. "You want to see my hat?" He began to pretend to look for the hat. "Is it under here?" He bent over to look under the car.

"No!" the girl squealed.

"Is it here?" He looked behind the girl's ear. She squealed again.

Hart froze. He knew what was coming now. He shrank back against the station wagon.

"Well . . . maybe . . ." Dub said, his hand on the door handle, "it's in *here!*" The rear door flew open. Out came the hat. Before Hart could catch his breath it was on Dub's head.

Ta ta ta ta ta TA.

Dub danced in the parking lot. His arms rolled in one direction. His hip threw out in the other direction. The fruit bobbed. The ribbons flew. The girl squealed

25

with delight. Hart's mouth dropped open at the horror of it.

The girl and the mother began to do the dance step too, and around them people stopped to watch.

Hart looked down at the pavement and communicated his displeasure the only way he could. He crossed his arms and tucked his hands into his armpits. His worst nightmare had come true.

Holy Mackerel!

"Holy mackerel!" Dub said. He whistled low and looked up at the coaster. He dabbed his forehead with his handkerchief as they snaked back and forth through the waiting line to ride the Jaguar.

A sign was posted beside the line: 30-MINUTE WAIT FROM THIS POINT.

The man in front of them turned around. "Hey, aren't you Dub Dugan, the weatherman?"

Dub's face seemed to light up. "Sure am," he said, shaking the man's hand.

Hart lowered his head. The dance in the parking lot had been bad enough. But at least the hat was safe back in the car.

"Say it for us," the man said. "You know."

Dub got a serious look on his face. He lowered his chin. He put his arms out.

"And th-a-a-a-a-a-a-t's the *wea*ther!" His voice boomed.

The people in line clapped. Hart felt the eyes of the crowd focus on them. He looked away. The line moved forward slowly. The wait seemed endless.

"Hey," Dub called out. "We need some action here!"

Hart's mouth fell open. What was Dub doing? He was yelling out like a camp director or something.

"Anyone remember 'Found a Peanut'?"

A few people laughed. "Found a peanut . . ." Dub sang. He waved his arms like a conductor. "Found a peanut . . ."

"Found a peanut just now . . ." The man in front of them joined in.

Two teenagers from the back of the line chimed in. "Just now I found a peanut."

Now the whole line sang. "Found a peanut just now . . ."

Hart focused on the coaster and tried to block out the singing.

"Cracked it open. Cracked it open."

The singing went on and on. As each verse began, more people joined in. The waiting line turned and they eased forward a few steps to take in a different view of the coaster. The vertical loop came into view.

Finally they reached the last verse: "Went to heaven just now." Dub bowed as the song ended and everyone in line applauded.

"Holy mackerel!" Dub leaned on the rail and looked

up at one giant loop of the coaster. "Hart, are you sure you want to ride that thing?"

Hart nodded. The line moved forward again. 20-MINUTE WAIT FROM THIS POINT.

"Twenty minutes," Dub read aloud. He turned back to the crowd. "Time for one more song. What do you say, folks? 'Ninety-nine Bottles of Pop on the Wall'?"

"Yeah!" came the response.

Hart moved away from Dub as far as possible in the tight line and tried to pretend that he was alone.

"Ninety-nine bottles of pop on the wall," Dub sang.

"Ninety-nine bottles of pop," the people sang back.

It wasn't until they were down to fifty-five bottles of pop that they walked up the wooden ramp into the loading station, past the statue of a cartoon jaguar holding up a yellow arrow and a sign that read YOU MUST BE THIS TALL TO RIDE.

"You think I'm tall enough?" Dub joked. "I know I'm wide enough."

Hart didn't laugh. He pressed ahead with the crowd. It was almost time now. He didn't like to admit it, but always right before a coaster ride he got a feeling in his stomach—a nervous twinge. He had the twinge now. His palms were just a little sweaty.

Dub was dabbing his forehead again and Hart saw his hand tremble as they lined up in the aisles. *One white-knuckler coming up!* Hart thought with satisfaction.

The Jaguar pulled up with a hiss, and suddenly it was their turn. They walked together to the train. Dub stepped back and held out his hand to help Hart get on. Hart stepped in. Dub hesitated, then shook his head and stepped away.

"You're not going?" Hart froze with his hand on the lap bar. He had never considered the possibility that Dub might not ride.

"I'll pass," said Dub. "I just remembered how much I don't like roller coasters." He stepped back and let out a deep breath, like a sigh of relief.

"But . . . you said you'd never been on one." As much as he did not want to be with Dub, anything was better than riding alone. Dub *had* to ride! "But—"

Snap!

The lap bar was shut. The attendant waved Dub away. "See you at the exit," Dub called out as the train rolled forward.

Hart's head jerked back, his mouth still open in surprise. As the coaster rolled forward, he had one last glimpse of Dub standing on the loading ramp. Hart stared at the empty seat beside him and realized that he had never ridden by himself before. It was too late to change his mind.

The twenty blue fiberglass cars jerked forward, then moved upward toward the 141-foot drop. Hart tightened his grip on the safety bar. He adjusted his back into the contours of the leather seat and tried not to think of the empty place beside him. He squeezed his eyes shut and let his head fall back onto the headrest. All the coasters that he had ridden so far had been with his father.

He leaned over the side of the car and looked down at the loading station. The people standing in line got smaller and smaller as the coaster climbed.

Hart could see Dub below. He stood just outside the exit gate talking to a small group of adults and young children.

Hart's father used to say, "There are two kinds of people in this world—carousel people and coaster people." The group at the exit gate were definitely carousel people:

A mother with a large diaper bag swung over one shoulder, jiggling a stroller back and forth. An elderly woman leaning against the rail watching the coaster, her hands clasped together as if in prayer. An overweight man in Bermuda shorts eating an ice-cream cone, his hand held under it to catch the drips.

And Dub.

He wondered if his mother knew that Dub had a bald spot on the top of his head.

Dub lifted his hand and waved. Hart did not wave back. Their eyes locked for a moment, and Hart imagined two laser beams coming from his eyes, fixing on Dub, and zapping him off the face of the earth like in a video game.

As the chain pulled up the coaster, Dub waved again.

Again! Was the man so stupid that he didn't recognize a laser-beam look?

The Jaguar jerked forward for the last time and eased over the hump at the top. Hart looked down 141 feet.

This was the only moment of a coaster ride that he hated. He could not change his mind. He could not get off. He could not change the course of the coaster ride. He could only sit helplessly and wait for the drop. The plunge that would take him to the finish.

"Here we go!" a voice yelled from the front of the train.

They dropped.

The train plunged down the first hill. The ground charged up toward them. Hart yelled. The wind whipped the yell from his lips, and for a moment he had the sensation of a free-fall drop.

His heart jumped in his chest. He willed his eyes to stay open and his arms to stay up. He could ride this coaster and he could ride it alone.

The Jaguar pulled out of the hill. The force of the pull-out pressed the riders down into the seats and slammed their heads back against the padded headrests. Hart's shoulders dipped, but his hands stayed high. The train whirled around a curve, and the seven loops swung into view.

"*Ooooooooo!*" the riders called as one, as the impact

32

of the view caught them by surprise. The wind pulled Hart's face into a tight smile. He was glad now that Dub was not with him. He did not need anyone.

Hart turned his head to the side for the first loop. Wind roared around him. He opened his eyes wide and forced himself to watch. He could see trees, flowers, and lines of people waiting for their turns to ride.

The trees, flowers, and lines of people began to rotate—around, upside down, and back. Before Hart could even yell they rotated again—around, upside down, and back.

Excellent.

The two side turns hit them before they were ready. No pull-out. No warning. They glided helplessly around the giant silver rings.

YEEOW!

One turn . . . two turns . . .

They whirled around the loops. The wind pulled back on Hart's face, but he kept his eyes open and looked down to the baseball caps and sunglasses in the grass below.

Next the spiral.

The grand finale.

Hart caught a glimpse of a trainload of upside-down people holding their hands up, screaming.

In half a second he was upside down too. Hands up, feet up, screaming, spiraling three times toward the end of the ride.

Hissssss.

The twenty cars rolled into the station. The brakes screeched as the cars jerked to a stop. The lap bars popped up, and the riders, weak-kneed and wobbly, began to get off the ride.

YEEOW! Hart added one more yell to cap off a perfect ride. He smiled at the attendant as he pushed himself up and out of the car. He had done it.

Without thinking, Hart punched the silver button on the side of his watch: one minute, forty-three seconds. As he stepped away from the car he was already rating the ride in his head. Twelve yeeows. Hart and his father rated coasters by the number of times that they yelled.

Dub was shaking each person's hand as they passed through the exit. "Congratulations, you lived," he was saying. Hart remembered the hat, the songs, Dub's face as the coaster pulled out, and his anger returned.

If he had to spend the whole day with Dub he would put the day to good use. Somehow, some way, before they left Wonderworld he would get Dub back.

Revenge of the Teacups

"Sorry I didn't go with you," Dub said.

"That's okay." Hart walked beside Dub.

"I get a little motion-sick."

The last thing Hart wanted to hear about was Dub's medical problems. "It's really okay."

"Let's put it behind us and have some fun," Dub said. "What next? How about the Runaway Mine Train?"

Hart shook his head. It was a kid's ride.

"How about this one?" They walked past the Flying Dutchman and watched the giant ship swing back and forth. The people in the rows of seats screamed as it rocked higher and higher.

Hart shook his head again. He knew what he was looking for. They walked on.

"How about that one?" Dub pointed toward a water ride. A large barge plunged down a waterfall, splashing the people inside.

It would be fun to see Dub get wet. Hart considered it for a moment, then shook his head. He had something else in mind. They passed a large sign covered with arrows. Each arrow pointed to a different ride. To the Thunderbolt. To Adventure Island. To the Dragon Fry. To the Twirling Teacups.

The Teacups.

Yes.

It hit him with its rightness. The Teacups looked like a baby ride, tame and gentle. It was, unless you had a tendency toward motion sickness. He rubbed his hands together. "This way." He led Dub in the direction of the Teacups. He walked faster.

"Holy mackerel," said Dub as they got in line. They watched the teacups go round and round, spinning in and out of view.

"You sure you want to go on this one?" Dub asked.

"You're coming with me, aren't you?"

"Wouldn't miss it."

Hart smiled. The Twirling Teacups. Frankie called them the barf buckets.

"This one doesn't spin too much, does it?"

"No," Hart said. "It's a baby ride. Look."

A teacup with a woman and two tiny girls swung into view. The girls' heads were pressed back against the woman. They swung out of view.

A woman in line behind them punched her husband

with her elbow. "It's Dub Dugan, the weatherman. That your boy?" she asked Dub, pointing to Hart.

"This is my friend Hart," Dub said, drawing Hart closer. Hart stiffened.

"Well, what do you think?" The man gestured toward the sky.

"Partly cloudy," said Dub, "strong chance of teacups." The man and woman laughed loudly.

Hart moved a few steps away. *Partly cloudy,* he thought, *strong chance of puke.*

The teacups slowed. People began to get off the ride. The line moved forward. "You sure you want to do this?" Dub asked again.

Hart nodded. They pressed forward with the crowd. "We got to get a good seat," Hart said. He led Dub to the outside teacups. The ones that whirled the hardest. Dub hesitated, then stepped into the green teacup. Hart stepped in beside him.

Hart watched the attendants load the teacups. One by one they helped the people in. Just as the last teacup filled, Hart made his move. "Oh," he said, "I just remembered how much I don't like teacups."

Hart jumped out of the teacup. He stood for a moment watching the surprised look on Dub's face. The surprise hardened into something else, and Hart looked away and hurried toward the exit. As he stepped out of the ride area the attendant pulled the lever.

Dub began to rise from his seat but it was too late. The motor hummed. The teacups jerked, and slowly they began to spin.

Hart grabbed the rail and looked for Dub. He felt his face flushing with pleasure as he realized that he had actually tricked Dub. Wait till he told his father about it. His father loved stories like this.

He strained for a sight of the green teacup. The cups whirled by, gaining speed, and within a few seconds the ride was in full swing. As each teacup passed Hart there was a loud *whoosh*.

Small children with parents. Children alone. Then the green teacup swung into view and Hart saw Dub, the only adult alone on the ride. His eyes were opened wide. His hands clung to the small steering wheel in the center of the teacup. Then he was gone.

Other teacups whooshed by. Blurs of red, blue, and purple. Other people whooshed in and out of Hart's vision. Screaming and laughing.

He spotted the green teacup again. This time Dub's eyes were closed. His hair had fallen over his forehead. His head was down on one arm and his face was a pale gray. He whirled out of sight again.

Hart had seen that color of face before. It was usually followed by someone throwing up. Dub wouldn't *really* get sick, would he?

An attendant passed. Hart grabbed his arm. "Hey, how long do they ride?"

The man shrugged. "We just let 'em go till the line builds up," he yelled over the hum of the ride.

Hart looked out at the line. There was no one there.

Suddenly he imagined his mother's face as Dub reported what Hart had done. His sense of elation dissolved as he realized it was his mother that he would have to face today, not his father.

All the consequences and possible punishments went through his mind as the teacups whirled. No TV for a week? The punishment for this might even be worse than no TV. Grounding? It might be worse than grounding. The worst consequence was one he could hardly even bear to consider: that his mother might give up on him the way she had given up on Kip.

Until his father left them, Hart had never realized that a parent could leave. But it had been so easy. One day his father's flannel shirts and jeans had hung in the closet, and his boots stood by the back door. Then they were gone.

After so many years of fights and tears, his mother had seemed to stop caring about his father. She didn't even try to get him to stay. "A person can only put up with so much," she had said to Hart.

He had to stop the ride. He had to stop the ride before Dub got sick.

Hart grabbed the attendant's arm again.

"I think that guy in the green cup is about to get sick."

The attendant looked out at the whirling cups. "Hey," he said, "isn't that—?"

The green teacup whirled into view. Dub leaned over and gagged. Then the teacup whirled on out of Hart's sight.

The man hurried over and pulled back the large lever. "Bummer," he said, then called to the other attendant, "Cleanup, cup three." The teacups began to slow now, winding down as the motor churned to a stop.

Hart scanned the cups for Dub. He spotted him on the far side of the ride mopping his white shirt with his cloud tie.

"You okay, mister?" The attendant took Dub's arm and helped him out of the teacup. Dub staggered toward the exit with his arms held out to keep his balance.

Hart stood by the gate. He hunched his shoulders and looked down at the pavement. Dub walked right past him. He walked slowly and unsteadily toward a bench beside the ride. Hart followed.

Dub sat down and mopped his face with his handkerchief. He brushed the hair from his forehead and patted it into place. He rested his head on the back of the bench and closed his eyes.

Hart's mouth was dry, and he could not possibly

have said a word even if he could have thought of a word to say. Around him there was motion and lights and laughter, but he was silent.

His mother had been so hopeful that he would get along with Dub. She would be disappointed. Anything was better than disappointing his mother.

His father used to disappoint her a lot. The worst time was right before the divorce. His father had been going to electronics classes at Tri-County Tech. He quit one day, but did not tell her. He left the house every day with electronics books and his lunch packed, pretending to go to the classes.

His mother had found out at the end of the month when the school called. Hart could still see her face and hear her voice when she had confronted Kip.

"You what?"

"I quit."

"Where have you been going every day? What have you been doing?" Her voice had become louder—as loud as Hart had ever heard it. "Why couldn't you tell me?"

Hart had never forgotten his father's answer: "Because I didn't want to disappoint you."

Hart had understood completely. He felt the same way. He was always hovering on the brink of disappointing his mother. How much disappointment would she take before she gave up on *him?*

When she read articles like "How to Help Your Child

Succeed in School," he felt unsuccessful. His C average must not be good enough.

When she read "Helping Your Child Make Friends," he worried that he didn't have enough friends. Actually he only had one: Frankie. That's the way he liked it— one friend you could trust.

Last week had been the worst. He found an article that she had been reading called "Does Your Child Need a Father Figure?"

He couldn't understand why his mother would think he needed a father figure. What was wrong with the real thing?

He also couldn't understand why his mother needed Dub. Were they in love? He thought about the way his mother looked at Dub, and he knew it must be true. Where did that leave Hart?

He eyed Dub. "I don't need a father figure," he told him. "I already have a father."

Dub opened his eyes. He looked tired. His earlier sparkle was gone. He looked directly at Hart.

"Your mother means a lot to me," he said.

Hart blinked. *That* he could understand. "She means a lot to me, too," he said.

Dub stood up. "I've had about all the fun I can stand today, Hart. How about you?"

"Yeah." Hart nodded at Dub. "Let's go home."

Dub rose from the bench and walked down the path that would take them to the exit. Hart didn't have any choice but to follow. He thought about his mother at home waiting to hear all about the trip. Dub would be sure to tell her everything. Hart beamed his laser eyes one more time at Dub's back.

If his mother and Dub were in love, then he was in trouble.

The Interrogation

"Did you have a good time?"

Hart's mother was waiting at the door. She had a half-clipped Lhasa apso named Daisy in her arms.

Hart shrugged. "Fine," he said. "It was fine."

"What do you mean, fine? You're home awfully early. Where's Dub? I expected him to come in." She shifted the wiggling dog and peered around the door at the driveway.

The interrogation had started. It reminded Hart of an old spy movie where the bad guys torture the spy to get information. He knew she wouldn't let up until he told her everything. But he couldn't tell her everything.

"He'll be back later," Hart said. He looked around to see how many dogs were left to clip. Daisy and a collie named Chesterfield were the only ones.

"Well, tell me everything you did."

"Mom." He gave her a warning look.

She looked into the upturned face of the Lhasa apso.

The Interrogation

"Daisy," she said, "he never tells his mother anything."

Maybe he should just tell her: *I made Dub ride on the Twirling Teacups and he barfed and had to go home.* Hart smiled.

"You *did* have a good time!" His mother's voice soared. "I see it in your face!" She looked down at the dog. "He had a good time," she said to Daisy.

"Mom!"

"Okay. Okay. Just tell me two things. Tell me the best thing about the trip and the worst thing about the trip."

Hart hated that. His mother had taken a class in parent/child communication. Now she always asked him that.

"The best and the worst," she said, staring at him. "Then I promise not to ask another question."

"Okay," Hart said. "But then no more questions."

"I promise. Come help me with Chesterfield. I've already brushed him out. He just needs his bath. We can talk while we work."

Hart followed her back to the room where she groomed the dogs. The black collie sat alone in a silver kennel. He trembled a little. His ears were pressed back. Hart looked at the door. This would be the fastest bath in the history of Sandra's Classic Clips. He reached in the cage, grasped the collie's neck, and pulled gently. "Come on, boy." He pulled the dog out.

Hart's mother put Daisy back up on the clipping

table and put a black strap around her neck. The strap attached to a metal stand that held the dog up in a standing position. She turned on the clippers.

"The best?" she said again. Strips of fur peeled away from Daisy's body as she worked. New, fresh fur was exposed.

"The best," he said, "was the Jaguar." That part was easy to talk about. "Length of ride: one minute forty-three seconds. The drop: 141 feet. Seven loops: two vertical, two horizontal, three spiral. Twelve yeeows."

His mother smiled at him from across the small room. "Well, how about the worst?" she called, over the buzz of the clippers.

Hart led the dog across the room and lifted him into the large dog sink. He turned on the water, adjusted the temperature, and began to wet down Chesterfield with the spray nozzle. Chesterfield stood resigned to his fate.

He couldn't tell about the teacups but he could tell about the hat. In fact, she needed to know about the hat. That would make her think twice about Dub, wouldn't it?

"Mom, he wore *it*."

"What?"

"The hat with the fruit on top. You know, the one he wears on sunny days on TV."

He waited for a word of sympathy, but nothing

came. "He wore it in the parking lot in front of everyone."

Hart looked up and saw that his mother was laughing.

"It wasn't funny," he said. "It was humiliating."

She covered her mouth with her hand. "I'm sorry. I didn't mean to laugh, Hart," she said, but her eyes were still crinkled with laughter. "It's just so, so, so funny. Tell me about it. I promise no more laughing."

"He danced, Mom. He danced in the parking lot."

She began to laugh again. "I can just see it," she said.

"It wasn't a pretty sight."

"Hart, that's just Dub. He wears that hat to the children's hospital to entertain the kids. He's the bravest man I know."

Brave!

Wearing a hat with fruit on it was not brave.

Chesterfield stood calmly, though his back legs trembled a little. Hart picked up a squeeze bottle of shampoo and squirted it on the dog's back. He began to rub the shampoo into a lather.

Hart's father was brave. He used to ask his father, "What's the bravest thing that you ever did?"

Every time he asked his father, his father had given him a different answer.

"Well . . . there was that time with the sharks. . . ."

Hart could still see himself as a child, his mouth open, hanging on every word.

"What time? What sharks?"

"But—you wouldn't be interested in that time."

"I would! I would too be interested."

"Nah, it might be too gruesome for a kid."

"No, it wouldn't! I promise it wouldn't! Tell me."

His dad would pause for effect and catch his breath as if he were about to begin the story. Then abruptly he would shake his head.

"No. No. I think it would have been the time during the war. Yes, the hand grenade . . ."

"What war? What hand grenade?"

"Well, I don't know if you—"

Usually at this point his mother would leave the room.

Hart could not remember ever hearing any of the stories. But he remembered thinking that his father was the bravest man in the whole world.

Wearing a hat in the parking lot at Wonderworld was not brave. He looked at his mother.

"Bravery and stupidity," he said to his laughing mother, "are easily confused."

"Hart, I'm just glad you two got along."

Hart watched Daisy's strips of fur peel away.

How did she get the idea that they had gotten along?

"Dub is taking me out to dinner tonight so I'll hear the whole story."

Hart stopped rubbing. "What?"

She turned off the clippers and picked up a wire brush. "Dub's taking me to dinner tonight so I guess I'll hear all about it."

"Frankie says you and Dub are . . . well . . . dating?" Dating sounded like such a weird term to describe your mother. He was sorry that he had said the word.

His mother paused. "You shouldn't believe everything that Frankie tells you," she said. "But this time he's right." The brush stopped in midair. "Hart, I've been seeing Dub for almost three months now."

"He's not very much like Dad. Dad's, well . . . fun. He rides coasters and stuff."

She looked up quickly. Now she began brushing harder. Quick stiff strokes. "You only remember your father on coasters. That's what you think of when you remember him. That's all you two do together. That's all you two can talk about."

Hart blinked. His hands rubbed the shampoo once and stopped.

A red blush was creeping up his mother's neck. "Do you remember him at Christmas?"

Hart shook his head. His chest tightened.

"How about your birthday? Do you remember him then?"

Hart shook his head again.

"How about your baseball games? Have you ever seen your father at even one of your games?"

She put down the brush with a smack. The conversation was over. She unhooked the black strap from Daisy's neck and picked her up.

Hart watched his mother walk out the door into the living room. His mouth hung open. He felt unbalanced, like a boxer who has been hit hard. He couldn't breathe for a moment.

She had never talked that way about his father before. They never talked about him at all. The things that she said weren't true. Were they?

His father hadn't been around much now for two years, and Hart and his mother had gotten along just fine. No problems. That had not changed. The only thing that had changed was that Dub was around. That was the problem. And that was a problem that Hart didn't know how to solve.

Viking Hats and Hula Skirts

Hart rinsed Chesterfield and put him back in the kennel. He adjusted the blow-dryer on Chesterfield's kennel and flipped the switch on. If he left now he would miss Dub.

There was a sharp rap and Hart heard the front door swing open. Too late. Hart stood in the doorway to the living room, feeling trapped.

"What a day," Dub said in his weatherman voice. He stepped through the door and wrapped his arms around Hart's mother and hugged her. Daisy dropped forgotten to the floor.

Dub was perfect once more. A clean shirt, combed hair. "What can I say, Sandra?" He hugged her again. "I have survived Wonderworld."

Hart's mother and Dub laughed together, not releasing their embrace.

Hart watched for a moment. Dub's hand came up to

his mother's cheek and brushed back a stray lock of hair.

Hart wanted to turn away, but he couldn't.

His mother looked over Dub's shoulder and beamed a smile at Hart. It was the kind of smile that she reserved for special moments—his class play, the rare A on his report card.

Hart's face burned. She thought that he and Dub had gotten along. She was proud of him. He couldn't stand it. Any minute Dub would tell her what happened. The house seemed too small.

"You should have seen Hart ride that coaster," Dub said. He winked at Hart.

"I wish I could have come," his mother said.

"The day would have been perfect if you could have." Dub leaned forward, and this time he did kiss her, right on the lips.

Hart took two steps back into the grooming room and stumbled over a towel on the floor. He couldn't believe what he had just seen. They had kissed right in front of him! Just a little kiss—but on the lips. This was serious.

He looked at Chesterfield trembling in his kennel and knew exactly how the dog felt. Hart couldn't escape now either.

He listened for a moment at the door. No kissing noises, just laughter. It was safe to come out.

"I'm going to Frankie's," he said, easing across the living room toward the front door.

There was no reply. His mother and Dub were sitting on the sofa. "It had three loop-the-loops!" Dub was saying, and then they both laughed. They were always laughing about something. His mother had laughed more in the last three months than Hart could ever remember her laughing.

He picked up his jacket. His coaster jacket. He rubbed his fingers nervously over the patches on it. THE SCREAMIN' EAGLE BATTALION. I SURVIVED THE WILDE BEAST. Patches that told of every coaster he had ridden with his father.

He backed slowly toward the door, unable to take his eyes off his mother and Dub. He reached the door and paused, waiting for an answer or some sign that he had been heard. Some sign that he existed.

There was nothing.

Bang!

He slammed the door behind him. He had seen enough, and he knew he would not be missed.

"Wait!"

The door swung open. Hart's mother stepped out onto the landing.

Hart froze halfway down the steps and waited.

"I'm sorry about what I said, Hart. I lost my temper."

"That's okay."

"It's not okay, Hart, and I'm sorry." She looked at him, obviously waiting for a reply.

Hart didn't know what to say. She wasn't saying that the things about Hart's father weren't true, just that she was sorry she said them. Was she waiting for him to agree? She didn't care about him anyway. She only cared about Dub.

"Daisy's ready. Will you walk her home for me on your way?"

His mother disappeared, then came out on the landing again with the freshly clipped dog. On Daisy's ears were two red-and-white checkered bows. She wiggled and strained against his mother's arms.

Hart reached for the leash. His mother put Daisy down.

Dub appeared at the door.

"What do you think?" she said, gesturing to Daisy.

He kneeled and rubbed Daisy behind the ears. Then he looked up at Hart's mother. "I think you're wonderful."

She blushed a deep red and beamed that special smile again, this time at Dub.

Hart walked down the steps without looking at them. He gave Daisy a pull and she followed. He had heard enough. The man was a fool.

"What do you think?"

"I think you're wonderful."

It was like the novels that Frankie's mother loved to

54

read. *Love* books, with titles like *Tender Torture* and *Pirate's Captive.*

He and Frankie had come across one that Frankie's mother had left forgotten in the hammock in the backyard. Frankie had picked it up and read dramatically from the back cover: "She was torn between two men: The aristocratic Lord Barnabas and the pirate rogue Devlin."

Mrs. Cambardella had come out and snatched the book from Frankie, swatting at them with it as they ran giggling away.

"I think you're wonderful."

The man had no pride. He would be no match for Hart's father. If only his father were here.

"Don't let her roll," said his mother, as he walked Daisy down the path. The door slammed shut.

Hart walked on the gravel shoulder of the road.

Dub brave? That was a laugh.

If he asked Dub, "What's the bravest thing that you have ever done?" what would he say?

He imagined Dub's answer like a cartoon:

In the first frame would be Dub in a wild Hawaiian shirt, with a bubble over his head. Inside the bubble it would say, "One time I had the courage to wear this shirt on the air."

In the next frame it would show Dub in a Viking hat. "One time I had the courage to wear this Viking hat on the air."

The next frame: "I had the courage to wear this hula skirt on the air."

The frames would go on and on.

Daisy sniffed at the weeds along the way. Hart pulled her along. They reached a small stretch of dirt on the side of the road.

"Roll, Daisy," said Hart. "Roll."

Daisy rolled over on her back and rubbed the newness of the haircut off into the powdery red dirt.

The Termite

"Hey, Hart, over here!"

He found Frankie in front of the McGinnitys' house inspecting a large pile of wood. Daisy had been delivered, and Hart was free for the rest of the afternoon. He wouldn't go home until he *had* to.

Frankie stood on the pile of wood and called to him: "How was it? The Jaguar!"

"Twelve," Hart answered. "A perfect twelve." He balanced himself on the pile of boards with Frankie.

"No kidding? A twelve?"

Hart nodded. "It was awesome. Two horizontal loops. Two vertical loops. Three spirals. We did some serious air time."

"How long of a drop?" Frankie asked.

"One forty-one."

"Wow. You are so lucky. What about Dub Dugan? How was spending the day with a celebrity?"

"Embarrassing." Hart sat down on the boards.

Frankie sat down beside him. "He embarrassed me all day. You wouldn't think that one person could find so many ways to embarrass you."

"You don't know my dad," said Frankie. "Adults are supposed to embarrass you. That's their purpose in life. I never told you about the time my mom and dad took us to Wonderworld?"

"You told me you went," said Hart.

"But I never told you what happened, did I?"

Hart shook his head.

"They sent us in and sat out front in folding lawn chairs, with a cooler of soft drinks between them, reading paperback books."

"You're kidding," said Hart.

"It's true," Frankie said. "Really."

"Unbelievable," Hart said. "How could anyone go to Wonderworld and not go inside?"

"Believe it," Frankie said. "My dad read *Spy Search*—the whole thing. Mom read *Love's Tender Furies*. I swear."

Hart gave Frankie a sympathetic look.

"That's not the worst. Nancy Zimmerman and Mindy Rigby saw them. They told everyone at school the next day. It was too humiliating for words."

"Today was worse than that. I *wish* he had stayed outside reading books," said Hart. "Dub wore that hat—you know, the one with the fruit, and he danced in the parking lot."

"Like this?" Frankie asked. He stood up, rolled his arms around each other, and threw his hip out to the side. The boards rattled, and he waved his arms to keep his balance.

Hart nodded glumly. "Then while we were waiting in line he sang 'Found a Peanut.' The whole crowd joined in."

Frankie winced. "Well, remember last year when my dad came to career day?" He began to select boards and toss them down from the pile as he talked. "He wore his old Navy uniform, and while he was talking three buttons popped off the front."

"I remember," Hart said with sympathy.

"One hit Mrs. Jenkins right between the eyes."

"My dad never embarrassed me," said Hart. "I always liked career day. My dad always had some great job that I could tell about. Like the time he worked on the shrimp boat, or the eighteen-wheeler."

"But he never *came*," said Frankie.

"So?"

"So, it's different telling about what they do. Like, I could have told some great stories about my dad being in the Navy but having him there in a too-tight Navy uniform is different."

"Yeah," Hart said. "I think I know what you mean. Remember when my mom came for career day?"

"Didn't she clip Mrs. Jenkins's poodle in front of the class?"

Hart nodded.

"Yeah." Frankie's face lit up. "Puff Puff got nervous and peed on Mrs. Jenkins's desk."

Hart cringed. "On the math papers."

Frankie thought for a moment. "Yeah," he said, "I think that might have been the worst. Nobody would put their math papers in their book bags. Everybody walked home that day carrying their papers with two fingers."

Frankie stepped down from the pile and picked up the end of one of the boards. "Come on, help me with this wood. We should be able to finish the Termite today."

Hart grabbed the other end of the board and lifted it. "Hey," he said. "The workmen told me we could have the *scraps*. These look too big to be scraps."

"Trust me," Frankie answered. "Would I ever lead you astray?"

Hart didn't even need to think about it. "There was the time in kindergarten that you talked me into jumping off your dad's toolshed with an umbrella," he said.

Frankie was silent.

"Remember this scar?" He pulled up the leg of his jeans to show Frankie the thin white line that ran down his ankle. "Fifteen stitches."

"Well," Frankie said, "we were young and foolish then. Was there any *other* time?"

Hart thought.

The Termite

"How about the time last year when we tried to build the swimming pool in your backyard while your parents were gone. I was grounded for a week."

"Okay," said Frankie. "I admit I might have led you astray that time. But can you think of three? I bet you can't think of three times."

"Well—" Hart began.

"Never mind," said Frankie.

The board bumped between them.

Hart thought back to the time in kindergarten that he had jumped off the toolshed. It had seemed like such a good idea. The umbrella would be just like a parachute. That's what Frankie had told him.

He remembered overhearing his father telling Uncle Mark about it on the phone.

"That's my boy. Yeah, went off a toolshed with an umbrella. Some kid, huh?" His father had been proud. He had made Hart tell the story of how they did it again and again.

Now even with his father gone, he weighed each experience and made each decision based on what it would sound like as he told his father. What would it take to make him proud again?

A voice in Hart's mind said, *"Some kid, huh? Built a coaster right in the back of the neighbors' yard."*

His father would approve.

Frankie led the way down the street to his house, then circled the backyard and cut through the hedge at

61

the back. They followed a path through the woods and came out by the ravine. It was a steep mountain slope.

They dropped the board on top of a pile at the crest of the hill. Frankie had been bringing boards all day. They sat down to catch their breath and looked out over the ravine.

The coaster had grown slowly over the course of three months. They had scavenged wood from every possible source. Hart made a weekly patrol down the street every Thursday before the trash pickup to pull out old pieces of wood from the neighbors' trash. One morning he had found a whole bookcase being thrown away. That had been enough wood to make ten feet of track.

Slowly, foot by foot, they had found wood, and the track had grown. Dub had helped in a way. The fact that his mother was seeing Dub had allowed Hart to build the coaster.

Since the divorce, she had wanted to know every single thing that he did. "Where are you going, Hart?" she would ask. "What's that in your hand?" she would say. "What did you do in school today?" The more questions she asked him the less he wanted to tell her. Since the day that she met Dub that had changed.

The questioning had shifted again. Once the questions had been directed at his father. They had been angry and accusing. Then, after the divorce, the questions had been directed at Hart. They had been worried kinds of questions, but not angry. Now she seemed more interested in questioning Dub. The questions to Dub seemed softer, not angry or worried but just interested. Like, "How was your day?" or, "Where did you have lunch?"

One morning Hart had walked through the house carrying a whole armload of wood, and she had not even asked what he was doing with it.

"Let's get to work," Frankie said. He stood up and brushed off his jeans. "If we hurry we can be finished before dinner and then . . ." He smiled at Hart.

"We ride!" they said together.

Sharks and Hand Grenades

"Over there a little more," Hart said to Frankie. "Yeah, nail it there." The coaster track had finally reached the bottom of the ravine.

There was no sound now but the steady beat of hammers as Frankie and Hart lined up the boards and nailed the strips down the center.

"Pass me more nails," Frankie called.

Hart passed the brown sack of nails to Frankie. As he hammered in the last few nails, Hart replayed in his mind his conversation with his mother.

It was true that his father had never been home for his birthday, not even before the divorce. Hart could not imagine his father singing as they gathered around a birthday cake. Before the divorce his mother used to cry on his birthday.

It was true that he had never been to one of Hart's baseball games. Sometimes Hart used to wish that one time his father could see him pitch. He tried to imagine his father sitting on the bleachers, cheering with the other parents, but he couldn't.

Hart could only picture his father riding coasters. The image in his mind was of a man with his hair blowing back, laughing into the wind.

But surely there was something that they talked about besides coasters. He thought, but nothing came to mind.

"Frankie?" he said.

"Yeah?"

"What do you and your dad talk about?"

"Hmm." Frankie stopped hammering and sat back on the grass. He seemed to be deep in thought for a moment. Then he answered, "Well, my dad goes, 'Clean up your room!'

"Then I go, 'In a minute.'

"Then he goes, 'I said clean up your room!'

"And I go, 'One more minute.'

"Then he starts counting like this: 'One . . . Two . . . Three . . .' "

"How far does he count?" Hart asked.

Frankie shrugged. "I don't know," he said. "I don't ever let him get past three. But that's our most common conversation."

Hart smiled. In his mind he could hear Mr. Cambardella's deep voice bellowing at Frankie. He always spent his free time at home, working in his rose garden, lying in his hammock with a book, cooking burgers on the backyard grill.

Hart hammered in the last nail on the last board. It might even be nice being yelled at if it meant having your father home.

They stood and looked up the hill at the track. "Perfect," Hart said.

"Let's finish the cart," said Frankie. "Then we'll try her out."

They scrambled back up the incline.

The cart looked a lot like a skateboard, only wider. Now Frankie found a board the perfect size. He unscrewed the wheels from his own skateboard to put on the bottom of it.

"See," he said, "we'll attach these wheels to that board. The board down the center will hold the wheels on the track."

Soon it was ready. Hart and Frankie looked down from the top of the ravine at the coaster.

"This is awfully steep," said Hart. "It doesn't look this steep on the blueprint."

"Faster ride," Frankie answered.

"And the cart," Hart continued. "The one on the plan looks a little . . . well . . . bigger."

"This one's big enough," said Frankie.

"Are you sure it'll stay on the track?" Hart asked.

"Of course," said Frankie. "It has to. If it didn't . . ." The sentence hung in the air.

Hart looked down the steep ravine. "If it didn't, a guy could get hurt," he finished for Frankie.

"Hart!" a voice called from the woods. "Where are you?"

"My mom!" Hart said. "If she sees this coaster she'll flip. She'll—"

His mother stepped out of the woods. She took one look at the coaster and her mouth dropped open.

"Hart*well*, you are *not* riding on that thing. You could hurt yourself."

"Mo-om."

"No, I mean it."

Hart inched toward the coaster as if to protect it.

"Mom, we won't get hurt. It's safe. We used a plan. Here. Look." He held up the blueprint.

"It is *not* safe. When did you make this? How could you have done this? Tomorrow we will come out here together and take these boards back."

"Mo-om," Hart pleaded.

"I have spent twelve years keeping you safe and alive and I'm not going to let you blow it now."

Hart sighed.

"Frankie Cambardella, your mother would not approve of this either."

Frankie's face was red.

Hart's mother turned and walked back toward the woods. "Come on, Hart," she said. "We'll discuss this some more later."

Hart turned to Frankie and raised his hands in a gesture of hopelessness.

Frankie mouthed the word *Tonight*.

Hart stopped, stared at Frankie, and nodded. They would ride the coaster tonight. Tomorrow would be too late. Tomorrow his mother would be sure that the coaster was destroyed.

"Okay, Mom," Hart said. "Let's go home."

He glanced one last time at Frankie.

Midnight, Frankie mouthed silently to Hart. Hart nodded to show that he understood and headed home behind his mother.

He would be back at midnight.

He followed his mother's brisk steps home.

"Mom," he said, trying to catch up. "Dad would let me do it. Dad's brave and he never got hurt."

His mother slowed down. She stared at him with the look that she gave her dogs when they came in for their clips—a sizing-up kind of look.

"Tell me," she said, "what exactly did your dad ever do that was brave?"

"Lots of things," Hart said. "There was the time in the war with the hand grenade . . ."

"Hart," his mother said sadly, "your father was never

in the war. There was never a hand grenade. Your father made that up."

"What about the sharks and the shipwreck? I suppose you're going to try to tell me that there was no shipwreck?"

She shook her head. "No sharks," she said, "and no shipwreck. I didn't want you to think badly of your father, but this is just too much."

"You're wrong. You don't understand us," he said, his face hot with anger. "Dad and me . . . We're alike. We're just alike. We're brave."

She stopped now and turned to face Hart. He couldn't look up in her eyes. She put her hands on his shoulders.

"Hart," she said, "I think one of the bravest things that I ever did was to marry your father. He was so wild and free, and we were going to backpack around the world and hang glide in South America and ride elephants in Africa."

"What happened?" Hart asked. He could see his father doing those things, but not his mother.

"You were born."

"So you couldn't go because of me."

"No, Hart," she said. "I stopped wanting to go. You were more important to me than trying to ride elephants in Africa. I think if your father were *really* brave he would have stayed with us."

She squeezed his shoulders, then let go and began walking briskly toward their house. Hart followed with brisk steps of his own.

They reached the front steps and saw Dub waiting in his station wagon. His mother looked at her watch and bit her lip. "Oh," she said, "Dub's ready to go. He's taking me out to dinner. Can we talk some more when I get home?"

Hart walked up the stairs. "We have nothing to talk about," he called back over his shoulder.

"Hart, think about what I said."

Hart slammed the door.

He leaned back against the closed door. How could his mother say those things? He didn't believe her. He remembered his father telling the stories, his blue eyes burning brightly, his smile big and full. Had his father been joking—*lying*—all that time?

He didn't know what was true anymore. He needed for his father to be brave. If his father was not brave then Hart was not brave either.

He decided he would forget the entire conversation.

No, he would remember *one* thing that had been said today, and that was the word *midnight*. He checked his watch.

Seven o'clock.

In five hours he'd show his mother what bravery really was. He would ride the Termite.

Broken Hart

Hart pressed his back against the door and listened. The car door shut. The engine started. The car drove away.

He had made his mother mad twice in one day—his mother who in the last two years had never showed her anger or raised her voice. She had taken an entire eight-week class one time dealing with parental anger.

There had been a lot of anger the year before the divorce, explosions of emotion and tears, and then after the divorce, strangely, no anger.

His mother had talked to dogs more in the last two years than she had talked to people. "You can trust dogs," she told Hart once. "They never disappoint you."

He had agreed. There was something comforting about the dogs. Before the divorce he had spent his weekends at the ball field, but since then he had preferred to stay at home. He worked every Saturday with his mother. There was a satisfaction in seeing the dogs change. They would come in dirty and shaggy, and they would leave perfectly clipped and groomed.

Since Dub had come into their lives, things had changed, and it was confusing. It was good to hear his mother laugh again, but now the anger was back too.

He walked back to his bedroom and sat on his bed. Would Dub tell his mother about today? He didn't think so. He remembered Dub's wink.

Hart reached under the bed and pulled out his shoe box. Under the pictures and newspaper clippings were three letters from his father. Hart thumbed through the envelopes, looking for evidence of his father's bravery. The edges were worn, he had looked at them so many times. He pulled out one of the letters.

> *Dear Hart,*
> *Great news. The trip's on for Kennywood.*
> *We're going to do it! Ride the big one. See you*
> *June 4. Be there or be square. Ha ha!*
> *Your Coaster Partner*

That had been the first trip—Kennywood Park in West Mifflin, Pennsylvania. Hart remembered how they had ridden a coaster called the Thunderbolt till midnight after the crowds were gone. Coasters sped up late in the night when the tracks were warm. The air seemed clearer then, and the lights of the other rides were spectacular from the view at the top.

But . . . He looked in the envelope one more time as if it might be hiding something else. It wasn't enough. He needed more. He pulled another letter out of its envelope.

Dear Hart,
  Coming at you. June 15. For......The Laser.
Can you do it! Yes!
                          Your Coaster Partner

Their second road trip had been to Allentown, Pennsylvania, to ride the Laser. It had been their first experience with the angled loop, a loop that turned you sideways. They rode for five hours. It had been drizzling that day. Perfect coaster weather! The rain kept the crowds away and sped up the ride.

But . . . he wanted answers. He needed his father to be here now. He looked at the last letter more quickly.

Dear Hart,
  Check it out. Coaster Magazine, *page 34.*
The Great American Scream Machine. Jackson, New Jersey. Pick you up July 7.
                          Your Coaster Partner

They had driven to Jackson, New Jersey, to ride a coaster called the Great American Scream Machine.

They had read in *Roller Coaster!* magazine about its boomerang effect. Its corkscrew was the best. It not only turned them head-over-heels but sideways at the same time.

But . . . he wanted to know what his father thought and felt. The letters didn't tell him anything about his father at all. He tossed the box of letters into the corner of his room and lay down and rested his head on the pillow.

If he closed his eyes, Hart could imagine himself with his father, riding in the MG and calling out coaster trivia questions, as they always did on their expeditions.

"Elvis Presley's favorite ride?"

"Too easy!" his dad would say, not looking up from the road. "The Zippen Pippen."

"Where?"

"Libertyland."

"Right." His dad never missed.

Hart would try again. "Coaster knocked down in *Smokey and the Bandit II*?"

"The Greyhound Coaster."

"Where?"

"Georgia State Fair Park, Atlanta, Georgia."

"Right."

His mother's words came back to him. *"All you two talk about is coasters."*

Hart tried to remember something else that they

had talked about besides coasters. There were the stories that his father used to tell, but now he knew that they were not even true.

Hart pulled out his coaster log and began to write in the information about the Jaguar.

>*Length of drop: 141.*
>*Duration of ride: 1 min. 43 sec.*
>*Comments:* For some reason that he could not understand, he wrote *Holy mackerel.*

He closed the book and stared for a moment at the cover. On the front it said *Roller coaster: A series of small open passenger cars that is pulled up on an elevated track, then drops, propelled by its own momentum.*

He pulled down his dictionary. *Coaster,* he found. *A person or thing that coasts.* He looked up *coast.* It said: *To continue to move forward after effort has stopped.*

Before the divorce there had been long phone conversations between his mother and father, always with tears and loud voices. He used to lie awake listening to the sound of her voice coming through his bedroom wall. Once he had heard her say, "You're breaking my heart," and for a moment Hart had thought that she meant him. Later he realized that she was talking about her own heart, but he held on to the image of himself broken in half.

After the divorce the phone calls ended, and so did the anger and hurt. He and his mother had just existed; he clipped the dogs, went to school, hung out with Frankie. Doing the same things that he had always done but without feeling. *Moving forward after effort has stopped.* It seemed to sum up Hart's life after the divorce perfectly. He had become a coaster.

He tucked the log book back under the bed. It seemed like days ago that he had been at Wonderworld. He lay back down, too tired to keep his eyes open. Without bothering to change into his pajamas, he closed his eyes and dozed.

A noise woke him. Outside a car door slammed. The front door creaked open and he could hear the muffled sound of his mother talking to Dub.

"No," she said. "I don't think I should tell him yet. He'll be so disappointed."

Hart stopped breathing. In one second he was wide awake. Tell who? What? He strained to hear Dub's reply.

"You know how he feels about his father," his mother continued.

Hart stiffened. How could Dub know how he felt? Right now even *he* didn't know how he felt. It bothered him that they had even discussed him.

"Well, maybe you're right. It's just going to be so hard on him."

The *who* must be Hart. But what was the *what?*

Dub mumbled something that Hart couldn't hear.

Hart heard a long silence and imagined a kiss. He squeezed his pillow and took a deep breath. To take his mind off the silence, he replayed the conversation in his mind:

"It's going to be so hard on him."

"His dad means so much to him."

It could only mean one thing.

His mother was going to marry Dub.

The Letter

Hart quickly turned off the lamp beside his bed. He scooted down under the covers, closed his eyes, and made his breathing regular.

He didn't want to talk to his mother tonight. He couldn't bear to hear the truth. She was going to marry Dub.

He heard her come into his room. He heard her pause. She must be looking at him. As usual she was probably checking to see if he was still breathing. Then she left.

Hart's eyes opened again. A feeling of panic rose within him. His mother and Dub married—his mind reeled at the consequences.

Would they live here? Would Dub even want him after what had happened today? How could she choose someone like Dub after she had been married to someone wonderful like his father?

He had always imagined that his father would reurn. That it would be like those romance novels that Frankie's mom always read.

Once he had asked Mrs. Cambardella about the books. He had been sitting in the Cambardellas' kitchen waiting for Frankie, when he had seen one of the books on the table.

On the front had been a woman and a man embracing. The man had wavy black hair, a patch over one eye, and a gun perched on one knee. He was dressed in buckskin clothes like Daniel Boone. Very small in the background was another man, wearing what looked like a pair of white tights and a powdered wig. His nose was pointed slightly into the air.

"Who gets the girl?" Hart asked, holding up the book.

Mrs. Cambardella laughed. "In these books the wild and daring guy always gets the girl," she said.

"Always?"

She nodded.

"That's the wild one, right?" Hart pointed to the handsome guy in the buckskins.

"Right," said Mrs. Cambardella. "But the girl tames him by the end of the book."

Now, lying in his bed, Hart imagined his own book jacket. The woman was his mother, not dressed in the jeans and sweater she usually wore but in an evening gown with flowers at the waist.

The man embracing her was his father, with his

wavy black hair and twinkling eyes, wearing his cow-
boy boots, jeans, and a leather jacket.

In the background, Dub. Dub in his suit and tie,
holding that little stick that he used to point to the
clouds on the weather map. He imagined Dub wearing
the hat with the fruit on top in the picture.

Torn between two men . . .

*Kip. The traveling rogue. Champion of the oil derrick.
Hero of the road. Captain of the* Mary Bee.

Or . . .

Dub. Mild-mannered weatherman on WBST.

Hart settled back into his pillow. His father might
not have combated sharks or tossed hand grenades but
he was still braver than Dub. Hart could not see Dub
driving an eighteen-wheeler, or piloting a shrimp boat,
or working on an oil derrick.

He needed to get the two men side by side. If his
mother could see them together, she would see clearly
the difference. He remembered Mrs. Cambardella's
words and they comforted him. *"In these books the
wild and daring guy always gets the girl. But the girl
tames him by the end of the book."*

Everything would be all right if only his letter would
come. If the letter came from his father, then he would
know where his father was, and could warn him about
Dub. Then things would turn out just as Mrs.
Cambardella said.

The clock blinked 11:45. All was quiet in the house.

The Letter

Hart eased his bedroom door open and tiptoed down the hall.

Almost time to meet Frankie, he thought as he headed into the kitchen and opened the refrigerator. He picked up a carton of juice, glanced once at the cabinet with the glasses, then drank directly from it, and put it back into the refrigerator.

His mother's purse sat on the kitchen counter. Beside the purse was a velvet ring box. Hart touched the soft top of the box, but did not open it. It was true. They were going to get married.

Sticking out of the purse was one corner of an envelope. It looked like hotel stationery. He couldn't breathe for a moment. He stared at the letter, his hand shaking just a little by his side, the juice suddenly curdling in his stomach.

Was this the letter he had been waiting for? And why had his mother not given it to him? He knew it hadn't come today because he had checked the mail himself. She'd had the letter for some time and had taken it to dinner to show it to Dub.

Now he knew.

They were going to get married and were trying to keep him from his father. He reached for the cream-colored letter, and he recognized the quick strokes of his father's handwriting.

The letter was addressed to his mother. Usually they were addressed to Hart. He pulled the envelope out of

his mother's purse and slipped out the single page.
Slowly he unfolded it and smoothed it out. He took a
deep breath and began to read.

> *Sandra,*
>
> *I'm off for the Caribbean today. Anchors away. Mark is the new social director for the cruise ship* Mardi Gras. *He's signing me on as his right-hand man. What a life! A year of dancing, dining, and playing cards, and getting paid for it. You have to admit I was always good for something! Ha Ha!*
>
> *Tell Hart hi. His dad's hit the big time! I'll send a postcard from every port. Won't make it this summer, I'll be cruisin'!*
>
> *Kip*

The letter crumpled in Hart's hand. He could not
move, he could not breathe. In the two seconds that it
had taken him to read the letter everything had
changed. His father was not going to help him.

He closed his eyes and tried to think. By now his father was on a ship in the Caribbean. He was already
sailing.

All the stories that he had planned to tell his father
had lost their dazzle. Tears came to his eyes; he
brushed them away.

What could he do?

The Letter

The painful answer was . . . nothing.

It was like that moment on a coaster—the one that he hated, when you pause at the top of the first hill. All the dips and twists and surprises lie ahead. You can't get off. You can't stop the ride. You can't do anything but wait for the drop. His mother, Dub, and his father were in control of the ride. He was not.

He dropped the crumpled letter to the floor. He wanted off the ride.

At least he could do one thing. He could ride the Termite. With new determination he pulled on his coaster jacket and slipped out the front door.

The Termite

The air on Hart's face was cold and a little damp. It was quiet outside. He pulled his jacket tighter around himself.

The street was dark except for the glow of an occasional streetlight. Hart jogged with determination in and out of the shadows and wished that he had thought to bring a flashlight.

One summer he and his father had visited an amusement park called Western World. There had been an entire village from the old West, complete with saloons, a general store, and a blacksmith shop. Every hour cowboys would have a gunfight on the street—a showdown.

When Hart had gotten on the chairlift to leave the village, they pulled up into the air and he had seen the backs of the buildings. They were propped up with long poles. They had no backs. The stores were just fake fronts made to look like real stores.

The Termite

His father, Hart thought, was like that in a way. He tried to be a real father by taking his son to amusement parks. But behind it all there was nothing. None of the things that real fathers did. No ball games and birthdays. No day-to-day conversations about things that mattered—just coasters.

Hart crossed the street and wished again that he had brought a flashlight.

The moon was bright, though, and if he stood for a moment and waited, it would appear from behind the clouds and he could find his way.

I've never done a single courageous thing in my whole life, Hart thought. *Except ride a coaster.*

He had ridden the Scream Machine, plunging down 160 feet into a seemingly bottomless pit.

And hadn't he ridden the Ninja, the black belt of roller coasters, skimming over a lake on a loop of steel?

Couldn't he ride the woodies with his hands raised high and feet up?

Hart sighed. Was that really brave? The coasters he had ridden were no more real than the fake buildings at Western World. They were only a series of false thrills and scares, designed to make you feel as if you were in danger.

He had been riding for two years—coasting over miles of track, screaming over nothing. For two years he had stopped feeling at all.

The Termite though . . . He shivered a little. It was real. It was not a regular coaster, not safety tested. It was something that he and Frankie had made by themselves. Only a truly brave person would dare ride it. He would prove his bravery tonight.

He hiked back through the woods and stopped at the ravine.

There it was. Beautiful.

He sat on a fallen tree at the top of the ravine and looked at the Termite. The moon illuminated the track.

He had been afraid it would look different when he got here. Like the pool that he and Frankie had tried to make in Frankie's backyard last summer.

When they had been working on the pool, it had seemed like a real pool. The vision in their minds of a blue rectangle had been so clear that it wasn't until Mr. Cambardella came home that they had seen it for what it was—a giant mud hole in the backyard where Mr. C.'s grass had been.

But the Termite was different. He was awed by it. It seemed just as terrific as it had earlier that day.

"Hey, Hart!"

He heard the crunch of footsteps and looked back into the woods. He saw the bobbing beam of a flashlight.

"Hey!" Frankie called. "You there?"

"Over here."

"Man, this gives me the creeps. It's so dark out here!"

Frankie came out of the woods and found Hart with the beam of the light.

"Wait for the moon," said Hart.

The cloud moved away and the moonlight returned.

Frankie sat down beside him on the tree. "You sure you want to do this?" he said.

"I'm sure."

Neither of them got up.

They stared out at the stars.

"We got to get our energy up first," Frankie said. He reached into a paper sack and pulled out two pepperoni rolls. He handed one to Hart and took a bite out of the end of the other.

"What's the bravest thing you ever did?" Hart asked abruptly.

Frankie thought for a minute. "Well, I guess it was the night that Jon Jon was born. I was asleep and I started to hear noises in the house. Like bumping and moving around. It was my dad sort of carrying my mother down the hall." He paused for a second to swallow a bite of his pepperoni roll.

"Go on," said Hart.

"My dad was still in his pajamas. He said, 'We've got to get your mother to the hospital.' "

"What happened then?" Hart asked.

"I tried to go with them, but my father said, 'Stay here, Frankie. We're counting on you to look out for your sister.' It was like a movie or something."

"You stayed?"

"Yeah," said Frankie. "You don't know how bad I wanted to go. My dad looked out the car window and said the two worst words in the human language: 'Be brave.' It was the longest night of my life."

"What did you do?" Hart asked, looking at Frankie with new respect.

"I played a whole game of Monopoly by myself. I bought Boardwalk. Then I paid myself rent. I moved all the pieces around. I passed go and gave myself two hundred dollars. It lasted till about three o'clock."

"And then?"

"Then I still couldn't sleep. I read this whole book of my mom's, *Color Me Beautiful*, and analyzed my colors. I'm a winter."

"Was your mom okay?"

"Yeah. They never told me she was having the baby. I thought she was dying."

"That was pretty brave of you, Frankie," Hart said.

"You gonna eat that?" Frankie pointed to Hart's pepperoni roll.

Hart shook his head. Frankie took it and bit off the end. "What about you?" he said between bites. "What's *your* bravest moment?"

"I don't think I have one."

"Everybody has one," said Frankie.

"I don't," said Hart. He set his jaw. "Yet," he added.

"Maybe this is it." Frankie pointed to the Termite.

"Maybe you're right," Hart said.

Frankie stood up and brushed the crumbs from his hands. "Where's the cart?" he said, shining the flashlight in wide arcs across the ground.

"Here," Hart said.

"Who's going first?" Frankie asked.

"I am," Hart answered.

One Yeeow

"Let's check the track first," said Frankie.

He moved down along the track, crablike in the dark, shining his flashlight along the expanse of boards.

Hart followed along behind Frankie, running his hand down the middle to check the board in the center.

"There's a piece missing here," he said.

Frankie hurried and brought another small board. They nailed it into place. The beats of the hammer echoed through the ravine. A dog barked in the distance.

Hart gritted his teeth.

Someone would surely hear them.

The sounds stopped, and they waited for a second in the silence.

"Everything else looks okay," Frankie said.

They were at the bottom, looking up at the track.

One Yeeow

The moon was shining, and they could see the entire coaster.

"It's pretty steep," Hart said.

"Let's try the cart once by itself," said Frankie. "Then if it's not going to work, we'll know it."

They climbed up the side of the hill. Hart had to place his feet sideways to keep his balance. He slipped and grabbed handfuls of grass to hold himself up as he climbed.

Finally they reached the top.

Frankie found the cart and they checked the bottom to see if the wheels were still in place. Hart fitted them over the center board and hoped that it would hold them on the track.

They stood for a moment at the top with Frankie holding the cart on the track. "Ready?" said Frankie.

Hart nodded.

They counted together.

"One . . ."

"Two . . ."

"Three . . ."

Frankie gave the cart a push.

They could hear a metallic rattling noise as the cart rumbled down the track—the sound of metal ball bearings and wood. There was a loud thud at the bottom.

"What was that?" Frankie asked.

"It hit something at the end."

Frankie gave a low whistle. "You better put your feet

down before you reach the end," he said. "You'll have to slow yourself down."

Hart nodded.

They scooted down the hill and retrieved the cart. They lugged the cart back up the incline and placed it at the top of the track.

Hart sat down on the cart. With his knees tight against his chest he barely fit on the small board. "I don't know if I can keep my feet on," he said.

Frankie found his paper bag and pulled out a fat roll of silver duct tape. Duct tape was an important part of everything that Frankie invented.

Frankie pulled off a long piece of tape and tore it with his teeth. He wrapped the silver tape around Hart's feet and the board, looping it three times.

"Now," Frankie said. "I think we're ready."

Hart looked straight ahead. The track seemed even steeper from this angle looking down. His stomach gave a twinge like he always felt at the top of a coaster ride.

He thought about the signs that they always have at the top of the first hill of a coaster. Signs like POINT OF NO RETURN.

"Ready?" asked Frankie.

No, Hart thought, he was not ready.

"Ready," he answered.

They began to count again.

"One . . ."

"Two . . ."

"Three . . ."

Frankie's hands pushed him forward. He was surprised at how fast he moved. The boards under him rattled as he gained speed. His fingers gripped the back of the board and he fought to keep his balance.

It worked! The Termite worked!

He soared down the ravine. Trees and bushes and rocks whizzed by him as he plunged downward.

"Yeeow!" he yelled.

Frankie ran along beside the track for the first few feet and then dropped behind. Hart was going too fast for Frankie to keep up.

The cart dropped forward, the boards rattled, the darkness closed around Hart, and there was only speed and motion.

He could not say later what went wrong. The board shuddered. The scenery flying by seemed to stutter. One second he was on the board. The next he was in the air. Then rolling and falling in a cheerleader's cartwheel without the grace, arm over arm over foot.

Crack! There was pain. A stabbing agony in Hart's arm, so strong that it left him weak and made his stomach heave. The shooting pain in his ankle told him it had been hurt too.

His body crumpled onto the hillside. More pain. Best not to move.

The cart dangled from his foot.

The skateboard wheels made a spinning noise; then there was silence.

"Haarrrrt!" Frankie's voice echoed over the ravine. Hart heard the scrambling noises as Frankie made his way down the steep hill.

"Wow!" Frankie was saying as he climbed down. "That was so cool! One yeeow! The Termite rated one yeeow!"

Hart couldn't answer. He heard Frankie crawl down the last few feet of the Termite.

"You okay? You okay?"

Hart still could not answer. He lay unable to speak. Unable to take a breath. Unable to move.

"Hart! Where are you?"

"Here," he said weakly.

Frankie reached him. He patted Hart on the face. "Hart, say something!"

"Ow," Hart answered with a moan. Finally he formed the words, "Get . . . help. Get . . . my . . . mom."

"Don't move," Frankie said. "Don't do anything." He twisted the bottom of his T-shirt. "Be brave," he added. Then Frankie disappeared up the side of the ravine.

Coaster Dreams

The darkness of the woods was complete.

Hart lay on a pile of leaves and twigs and stared out into the night. He blinked his eyes. There was no change. It was just as black. He had lost his glasses in the fall.

He imagined Frankie running for help. It was at least half a mile back to their neighborhood. Running was not Frankie's best skill. Frankie was the only kid in his class who took longer than twenty minutes to run a mile. He had failed the Presidential Fitness Test. How long would it take Frankie to bring help?

Hart thought of his mother asleep in bed. He thought of all those cartoons with bleached white bones in the desert. She would be sad if he died. All those parenting classes down the drain. He smiled for a second, but a new wave of pain wiped the smile from his face.

"Aww!" He moaned again.

Hart gently touched his hurt arm. He ran his fingers from the shoulder down the arm and felt bone protruding from the side of it, and moisture—blood. Maybe he *could* die.

His stomach heaved again and a wave of nausea overcame him. His head spun and he fought to stay conscious. He squeezed back tears and looked up the ravine.

The moon emerged from behind a cloud and shone down, illuminating the long snaking board track that he and Frankie had created. His own words came back to him: *"Courage and stupidity are easily confused."*

He struggled to stay conscious.

Suddenly he was not lying on the ground at the bottom of the ravine but was back on the Wild Side, resting his hands gently on the lap bar. Out and back he rode.

The pull up the lift hill, and out—over the park, down the first hill, the helix, the second hill, the tunnel, the curve beside the ocean. Then back—down the last hill and into the station. Out and back. Over and over.

The drumming of the wheels on the tracks, the pull of the ratchets, the screech of the brakes. He rode on, hypnotized by the rhythm of the coaster.

"Hart!"

In the dream someone called his name.

"Hart, over here!"

He looked up and saw his mother standing beside

the turnstile. He froze. Dub was beside her. In the dream he wore the hat with the fruit on it.

Out he went again. The coaster sped up and he could not get off. He spun round and round till the coaster became a whirling teacup. He kept reaching out of the teacup for someone to help him get off. His father whirled into view, then out. His mother and Dub stood on the sidelines and watched. He listened to the screams around him. He opened his mouth and screamed.

Thunder rumbled in the distance.

Hart's eyes blinked open. Where was he? Darkness was all around him. Above, the stars twinkled.

He tried to sit up and a wave of pain hit, and he remembered. The ravine. The coaster. How long had he been out? He was trembling uncontrollably. He could not stop.

The weather had changed; the night was cold. Hart shivered in his thin jacket.

Come on, Frankie, he thought. *Don't let me down.*

The thunder sounded closer now. A crack of lightning lit the sky. Hart squeezed his eyes shut.

It was useless to yell. It was impossible to crawl up the steep slope. He prayed. *Let Frankie come.*

Faintly in the distance, like a dream, Hart heard a voice. "Hart!"

And again: "Hart!"

He had wished for so long that he would hear his name that he thought it *must* be a dream.

It was so far away.

"Hart!" The voice moved closer.

It was not a dream. It was his mother's voice.

"Help!" He tried to yell but the word came out in a whisper.

He could hear talking. He could hear Frankie.

"This way, Mrs. Patterson. Over here!"

Hart opened his eyes. Frankie had brought his mother. He could hear them closer now, moving toward him.

"Hart? You okay?" Frankie reached him first, scrambling down the ravine.

The rescue was like film clips going in and out of focus. Over it all was a calm voice, a steady voice, that gave directions and took control.

"I'll go first, Sandra." Dub's voice.

Hart lay back and closed his eyes. Dub had come too. He was glad. Somehow he knew that Dub would know what to do—how to help him.

"Here, Sandra, take my hand."

Then, miraculously, his mother was with him. "Hart?" she said. She knelt beside him and held his hand.

Dub knelt on the other side. "We've called the ambulance, Hart," he said. "They're on the way. Mr. Cambardella is up at the street to show them where we are."

His mother's hand brushed his forehead. It was warm. He closed his eyes.

"Don't try to move, Hart," Dub said gently, adding in a calm voice to Hart's mother, "It's better not to move him until the medics come."

In the distance they heard a siren.

"What's that?" Frankie's voice asked.

"That's a bone," said Dub. "Sandra, help that kid."

"What kid?" he heard his mother ask vaguely.

"Him. What's his name?"

"Oh. Frankie."

"He just passed out."

Through the pain Hart smiled just a little. Then he let go and drifted into the blackness around him.

Bad Breaks

The hospital room was white and blue everywhere Hart looked. Sunlight came streaming through the window.

Hart's mother sat in a small vinyl chair reading a pamphlet called *Understanding Your Adolescent*.

"Mom?" he said. His mouth was dry.

"Hart. You're awake." His mother leaned over from the chair to pat his arm. She looked tired; there were dark circles under her eyes. She wore jeans, her "I ♥ collies" sweatshirt, and bedroom slippers.

"Mom," he said again. His voice cracked.

"Don't talk, Hart. You've had a hard night." She picked up a small plastic pitcher from the nightstand and poured water into a cup. "The doctor says you need to rest. You'll be fine."

She put a bent straw into the cup and held it to his lips.

Hart lifted his arm but realized there was a long tube

attached to it with a needle. He put his arm carefully back down.

"That's for infection," his mother said as he drank. "That was a bad break." The other arm had a large blue cast on it.

"My leg?" he asked. He moved it a little but it hurt, so he stopped.

"It's just a sprain," she said. "You were lucky."

Lucky was not exactly the word that Hart would have chosen.

"I'm sorry, Mom."

"It's okay, Hart. Everything's okay."

"Have you been here all night?"

She nodded. "Dub's been here too," she said. "He went downstairs to get me some coffee."

Hart closed his eyes. He felt a sense of relief that his mother was not alone.

The phone rang. His mother answered and talked for a moment.

"It's your dad," she said. "He's calling from Saint Thomas. Do you feel like talking to him?"

Hart reached too quickly for the phone. Pain knifed through him. "Ouch," he said.

He closed his eyes for a second while his mother stood up and placed the phone to his ear. He reached up slowly with his good arm and held the phone in place.

"Hart! Hart, you there?"

He heard his father's booming voice coming through the phone lines as if he were right there beside him.

"What happened, Hart?"

"Frankie and I," he began. "We built a coaster down the side of the ravine."

"You what!"

"We built a roller coaster." He told his father the story.

"Wait a minute. Mark, come here, you gotta hear this!"

Hart heard a shuffling around as his father adjusted the phone.

"Now tell me again."

Hart told the story for Uncle Mark. Then his father got back on the phone.

"How did you do the duct tape?" his father asked. "Barney," he called to someone else, "listen to this. This is my boy. Built his own roller coaster and rode down a ravine. Some kid, huh?"

Hart's arm throbbed. The phone was too heavy.

He moved his shoulder and the phone dropped. His mother picked it up.

Hart closed his eyes and listened to the one-sided conversation.

"He's tired," she said.

Then: "I'll ask him later." She hung up the phone.

"What did Dad want you to ask me?" Hart said.

"He asked if you wanted to ride the Cyclone with him next summer."

"Oh," Hart said. "I can't think about coasters now."

"I don't imagine so."

"Mom?"

"Yes?"

There was something that he wanted to say but he couldn't put it into words. He was drowsy from the medicine. It was a feeling that overwhelmed him, that he could not describe—the feeling had something to do with having her here. But he couldn't find the words.

He wanted to tell her how glad he was that she was here with him. That he was glad that she had not gone hiking around the world or hang gliding in South America or riding elephants in Africa. That he was glad that she had stayed to protect him from plastic bags and mayonnaise. That's what he wanted to tell her. But he didn't even know how to begin.

"Mom," he said instead, "remember the time you clipped Mrs. Jenkins's French poodle, Puff Puff?"

"What?"

"Remember on career day, at my school."

"Oh," she said. "Now don't start worrying about that. I know how upset you were. I'm sorry."

"It's okay, Mom," he said. "I'm just glad that you came."

Pepperoni Rolls

Hart's mother had put up a banner from her clients across the wall of the hospital room. It said GET WELL, DOGGONE IT! There were paw prints all over the sign with names beside each one: Daisy, Tobie, Midnight, Chesterfield.

There was a card from the TV station, with a bunch of balloons. It had a cloud with a sad-looking face on the front of the card and said, *Sorry you're under the weather!*

Frankie had sent a card that said *Fifty Things to Do While You're in the Hospital.* Hart had already tried two: *See how many words you can make from the letters in the words* hospital gown; and *Tap out the rhythm of the* Addams Family *theme on your nurse call-buzzer.*

"You're a friend of our celebrity, I hear," the nurse said as she opened the blinds. She nodded toward the balloons. "We all love Dub here at the hospital. Have

you ever seen that dance he does? *Ta ta ta ta ta TA!*"
The nurse did a little dance step.

Hart nodded. He didn't want to think about Dub. He had not seen Dub since the accident. Dub had not come in to see him. Every time he heard Dub come down the hall he closed his eyes and pretended to be asleep. Every time Hart thought about Dub he remembered the whirling teacups and he felt bad.

"You need anything, Hart?"

"No thanks," he answered.

"Just push the buzzer if you do. Once is plenty."

"Okay."

"I'll be down the hall if you need me, Mrs. Patterson," she said to Hart's mother as she left the room.

Hart sat up in bed and flipped the remote-control button to change the channels of the small TV.

Click, click, click. There was nothing on but talk shows. He was bored with the hospital and tired of hurting. He understood now why kids liked hospital clowns. Any entertainment was welcome. He remembered Dub telling him about the kids who needed cheering up, and now suddenly he was one of them.

He heard the rolling lunch cart in the hall. What would it be this time? Beef broth or Jell-O? He wasn't hungry anyway.

"Anybody home?" Dub's voice called out.

Hart closed his eyes but not fast enough.

"Hey there, Hart." Dub stopped the lunch cart just outside the room. It was covered with a sheet, and the hat with the fruit was on top of it. "I brought you something."

"I'm not hungry."

"You'll like this." He pulled back the sheet and from under the cart came Frankie.

"*Ta da!*" Frankie said.

"Dub!" Hart's mother said, rising from her chair. "He's not allowed in here."

Dub pressed his finger to his lips. "It helps to be friends with the nurses," he said. "They said it would be okay as long as you guys don't throw any wild parties."

Hart's mother smiled. "Thanks, Dub," she said.

Hart didn't know what to say. He was so thankful to see Frankie that he almost cried.

"Hi," was all that he could come up with.

"Come on, Sandra," Dub said, picking up the hat. "I'm going to visit some friends. We'll be back in ten minutes," he added. They walked down the hall, and Hart could hear his mother laugh at something that Dub said.

"Awesome bed." Frankie walked over to the bed and sat down. "What does this button do?" He pushed a button on the side of the bed. The bed went up. "Cool!" He pushed another button and the bed went down. He laughed.

"Ouch!" said Hart.

Frankie stopped laughing. "Sorry," he said. "Does it hurt?"

Hart nodded.

"A lot?"

"A lot," Hart answered.

"My cousin was in the hospital," Frankie said. "She told me the things that doctors say, that you need to look out for. Because they say one thing and it means something else."

"Like what?"

"Like, 'This is going to make you a *little* uncomfortable.' That means that they are going to do something to you that *really* hurts."

"I heard that one already," Hart said. "And your cousin's right."

"Or this one," Frankie continued. " 'You'll feel a little pinch now.' That means they're about to jab you with a needle."

"Don't make me laugh, Frankie. It hurts too much."

"Man," said Frankie, "I didn't think we'd get hurt or anything."

Hart nodded.

"My dad made me take all the boards back. He made me take the cart apart too. The Termite is gone." He stared at Hart for a moment. "You look better than the last time I saw you," he said. "Last time I saw you, you looked awful."

"It's strange," said Hart. "I can remember some things about that night but I can't remember others."

"It was crazy," Frankie said. "I ran all the way to your mom's house. She called Dub, and by the time we ran past my house, Dub was pulling into our driveway. Dub said he drove through three red lights to get to you. He looked pretty worried."

"He did?"

Hart remembered Dub's hands on the steering wheel driving to Wonderworld. He had so carefully slowed and stopped at every stop sign. It was hard to imagine Dub running stoplights to get to him.

"He said he even passed a police car, doing fifty miles an hour on a thirty-five-mile-an-hour street." Frankie paused, looking worried himself. "You remember anything else? Like about me?"

"You fainted."

Frankie blinked. "Well, I wouldn't exactly call it fainting," he said. "I mean sometimes a guy's got to rest his eyes, you know."

Hart smiled.

"You hungry?" Frankie asked.

Hart nodded, surprised to discover that he was.

"You'll never guess what I brought." Frankie reached behind his shoulder and swung a backpack forward. He pulled the flap open and pulled out a plastic bag. "Pepperoni rolls," he said.

Frankie opened the bag, and the aroma of pepperoni

filled the room. "My mom made them this morning. They're still warm," he said, sniffing the air.

"Hey, guys," Dub called from the doorway. "Time's almost up."

Hart looked up at Dub, who stood beside his mother. He seemed to tower over her, large and solid. He held the hat with the fruit on it. For some reason it didn't bother Hart anymore.

He wanted to thank Dub for helping to rescue him and for bringing Frankie today. He wanted to say that he was sorry about the teacups. But Frankie was there and so was his mother and he didn't know how to say it all anyway.

He wondered if his father had this problem. You couldn't always say what you wanted to say. Sometimes something else just came out instead. Maybe the coaster talk meant something else. Something his father couldn't say. Like body language or the way doctors talk, saying one thing that means something else.

"You like pepperoni rolls?" Hart asked Dub instead.

"I never had one," Dub answered.

"You want one?"

"I'd love one."

"Come in," said Hart.

Dub tossed the hat onto the lunch tray and walked into the room.

The Ring

"Open up!"

Frankie knocked on Hart's bedroom window. He cupped his hands and pressed his nose against the glass.

Hart reached over and turned the latch and tried to pull it up. His arm was almost completely healed now but the blue cast kept him from lifting it.

"Help me out," he called.

Frankie pulled on the outside of the window and it slid up and open. He climbed in. "Hide me," he said. "I'm desperate! My mom's working me to death. I don't know why your mom had to get married at my house. I had to cut the grass, trim, *and* edge."

Hart sat back on the bed and picked up a large black shoe. He held it between his knees and polished it with a soft cloth. "Hide *me*," he said. "Weddings are a lot of work."

"So I noticed," said Frankie. "Did you hear about the

man who married three women in one day?" He sat down on the bed beside Hart.

"Come on, Frankie, we don't have time for your stories. My mom's getting married in two hours."

"Just think about it. A man marries three women in one day."

"I've got to shine these shoes for Dub, then get dressed, then go get pictures taken."

"Give up?" Frankie said.

"And I've got to . . ." It was no use. "Okay," Hart said. "How did he marry three women in one day?"

Frankie grinned. "He was a minister. Get it? He *married* three women in one day."

"Ha ha ha." Hart smiled despite himself. "Now help me polish these shoes."

Frankie picked up the other shoe and began to rub it with the edge of the bedspread. "I can't believe it," he said. "I mean, your mom is going to be Mrs. Dub Dugan in two hours."

"Believe it," said Hart.

"You're practically a celebrity. Do you think any news reporters will come?"

Hart shook his head. "They want it to be a quiet wedding," he said. "Just your folks, some people from the TV station, and the neighbors. And some dogs."

"Dogs?"

"Yeah, my mother's got to be the only person in the world to invite dogs to her wedding."

"Maybe we can get her into the *Guinness Book of World Records*—most dogs at wedding."

"I don't think that would fit in with her idea of a quiet wedding," said Hart.

Frankie looked at Hart rubbing polish on the black shoe. He turned the shoe that he was holding over to the bottom. "One time at my cousin's wedding someone wrote 'Help me!' on the bottom of the groom's shoes. Then when he kneeled for the prayer . . ."

"Don't even think about it," said Hart, looking down at the shoes.

"Dare you?"

Hart shook his head. "Not this time."

"Hart!" his mother called from the living room.

"Yeah, Mom," he called back.

"Have you seen Frankie? Mrs. Cambardella's on the phone."

Frankie pressed his finger to his lips and moved toward the window.

"Frankie's not here, is he?"

Frankie slipped out just as Hart's mother opened the door.

"No, he's not here," Hart answered.

"That's what I told her," she said. "You about ready?"

Hart stared at his mother. She looked different. Her jeans were gone and she stood in the doorway in a long blue dress that he had not seen before. Her hair was fixed up on her head with flowers. Just like the heroine in Mrs. Cambardella's novels.

"Mom, you look . . ." He struggled to think of the right word. "Different."

She smiled. "Thanks." She stood and looked at him for a moment. "You look different too." She sat down beside him and rubbed his hair. "You look a lot like your dad today."

He looked up into the mirror and saw his dad's square jaw and wavy black hair. He pushed his glasses up. "I look like Dad," he said. "But I'm not like Dad."

"I know," she said.

"Why did you marry him?"

"The day I married your father was one of the happiest days of my life. I loved him . . . and . . . I thought I could change him, like I change my dogs. It took me a long time to realize that he could never be what I wanted him to be."

"Which was?"

"I guess it was . . ." She paused and shrugged. "Well, I guess it was *here*. I wanted him to be *here*."

Hart nodded. "Me too," he said.

Mrs. Cambardella's rose garden was clipped and pruned. The grass was cut and edged. The food was waiting on long tables at the side. At the end of each table was a silver bowl of dog biscuits. Everything was ready.

Daisy, the only bridesmaid, wore white lace bows, and a Border collie carried a small basket of flowers down the aisle to an arbor of roses where Hart's mother and Dub stood.

Hart stood beside his mother. The minister was reading the vows out of a small black book. Hart looked over at Frankie across the lawn. Frankie crossed his eyes. Then he grinned.

"The ring," said the minister, looking at Hart. "The ring, please."

The ring? Hart reached into his pocket and hoped that the ring was still there. It was. He gave a sigh of relief and pulled out the golden wedding band.

Everything seemed unreal for a minute. Like the beginning of a coaster ride—the unknown stretching out, waiting to be experienced. It was scary.

Dub looked nervous in a black tuxedo, his only touch of gaiety a Dalmatian-spotted tie. His mother smiled in her long blue dress.

This, Hart thought, *is my bravest act*. He took a deep breath and handed the ring to his mother.

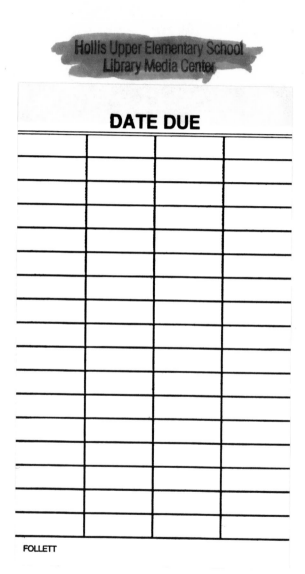

Hollis Upper Elementary School
Library Media Center

DATE DUE

FOLLETT